John Kirkwood Leys

The Lindsays - A Romance of Scottish Life

Vol. II

John Kirkwood Leys

The Lindsays - A Romance of Scottish Life
Vol. II

ISBN/EAN: 9783337051815

Printed in Europe, USA, Canada, Australia, Japan

Cover: Foto ©Andreas Hilbeck / pixelio.de

More available books at **www.hansebooks.com**

A Romance of Scottish Life

BY

JOHN K. LEYS

IN THREE VOLUMES
VOL. II.

London
CHATTO & WINDUS, PICCADILLY
1888

CONTENTS OF VOL. II.

THE LINDSAYS.

CHAPTER XIII.

SOPHY MEREDITH.

In a garden, the garden of a large old-fashioned house on Highgate Hill, a girl sat with a book in her hand, dreaming, on a July afternoon.

The scene was a thoroughly English one. Behind the garden-seat rose the gray brick walls of the house. It was old without being in the least degree venerable, ugly without looking positively mean. Its size redeemed it from that—its size, and a certain air of comfortableness that belongs only to English homes. High walls shut out the sight of the

new garish houses of red brick, and the
sounds from the road, which of late years had
become very much like a street. Within the
lofty garden walls, order, comfort, propriety
were supreme—they were not likely to be replaced by any other principles so long as
Sophy Meredith reigned at Grove House.
The lawn exactly resembled a carpet; not a
weed was to be seen in gravel-walk or in
flower-bed; the rose-trees had just so much
liberty as would prevent their appearing
formal, not a fraction more. But the
principle of order was, after all, subser-
vient to that of comfort. Books and
magazines, garden - chairs, and bits of
feminine 'work' lay about. On one side
stood an invalid's chair.

Sophy lay back on the garden-seat, her
hands clasping the half-closed book on her
lap. She was no longer a girl, being now
seven-and-twenty; but she had one of those
smooth, fair complexions which take ten years
off a woman's apparent age. Her features

were not striking, but very pleasing, and suited well her slight figure and her low fore-head.

As if unable to sit still any longer, she rose and passed into the house through a French window which was standing wide open. The drawing-room, like the garden, spoke of orderly comfort. Everything was in its place, yet one could not say that the room or its furniture had an air of stiffness. Cross-ing over to the mantelpiece, Sophy lifted a letter-weight which had been placed above some neatly folded papers, and took from under it a telegram. She blushed slightly as she opened it, for she knew it by heart already. It was dated on the previous evening, and contained only the words : ' Shall be with you to-morrow afternoon.—Hubert.'

This quiet dwelling was Hubert Blake's home, the only home, at least, that he had ever known, though he generally lived in his chambers in London. His uncle, who had been his guardian, was now an old man and

19—2

an invalid, or rather, a valetudinarian. He
had been for the last ten years a widower;
and Sophy Meredith, his wife's niece, had
managed his household and seen to his
comfort since his wife's death. Hubert and
she had been, of course, thrown very much
together. They called each other 'cousin,'
though they were not really related to one
another, and corresponded at intervals, sometimes in long, chatty epistles, oftener in brief
notes.

Four years had passed since Hubert had
despatched those long letters from the Castle
Farm ; and for the last two years the in-
mates of Grove House had heard very little
from him. He had been wandering over the
face of the earth, trying to find occupation,
excitement, anything to drive Margaret Lindsay's image out of his head.

After meeting her at Arrochar three years
ago, he had thought himself cured of what he
told himself was a halfinsane passion. He
saw plainly that Margaret was not suited to

him. Her mental powers, though considerable, were totally undeveloped. The world
of literature and that of art were as unknown
to her as the world of fashion. It would be
an act of folly, he knew very well, to tie himself to one with whom he had so little in
common, and who was so little likely to be
moulded by any man as Margaret Lindsay.
So he did not follow her back to Castle Farm.
He stayed at Arrochar for a few days, and
then wandered westwards.

But the girl's face haunted him. At times
he was consumed with a desire to make this
stately, simple, self-sufficient beauty his own,
to feast his eyes continually on her loveliness,
to watch her unfolding mind as she was
brought into new scenes and surrounded with
new ideas. He felt as if he could not live
without seeing her again. Accordingly he
ran down to Scotland a third time, and
(under cover of his friendship with her
brother) spent some days in her company.

But her presence did not satisfy him. She

was cold, narrow, unsympathetic, as she had always been. He went abroad, determined to stay away till he should forget her. Now, at last, he was coming home.

Sophy, having read the welcome telegram two or three times, as if to assure herself of its truth, replaced it under the paper-weight, and then left the room, going into the hall. Opposite her was a broad flight of shallow steps, and these she ascended. Going a little way along a corridor, she came to a door, which she softly opened. It led to a large bedroom with a wide window, which commanded a view of the greater part of London; this was the room which Hubert always occupied when he was at Grove House.

With something that was not exactly a blush, Sophy moved noiselessly from the dressing-table to the writing-table, seeing that nothing had been omitted. Everything was in its place; everything was spotless and fragrant. There was nothing to be supplied, nothing to be altered; and yet the girl looked as if she must do something. She went back to the garden, picked a single red rose, and then, going up to the second floor, she visited her own bedroom, and took out of a closet a slender glass vase. It had been presented by her to Hubert long ago; boy-like, he had forgotten it, and, indeed, it was not a very suitable present for a lad. Sophy took the neglected vase, placed the rose in it, and carried it down to her cousin's writing-table.

She was leaving the room when she heard a querulous voice calling her, and she hastened to the end of the corridor, and entered Mr. Blake's sitting-room. He was a thin, tremulous, dried-up looking old man, who looked as if he were in a state of perpetual anxiety.

' Is that you, Sophy ?'

' Yes, uncle.'

' Has Jackson gone with the brougham to meet Hubert ?'

' Not yet, uncle.'

'Not yet! Why haven't you sent him off?'

'The train is not due till 5.30.'

'Let him go at once!' interrupted the old man. 'I wouldn't have him late on any account. I wonder, Sophy, you haven't more consideration for Hubert, when he has been so long away, than let him run the risk of finding no one to meet him at the station.'

Sophy turned away to carry out her uncle's wishes with a half-sad, half-contemptuous smile about her lips.

The afternoon was a tiresome one, but it wore itself away at last; and the carriage made its appearance. Before it had time to stop, Hubert sprang out and grasped his uncle's hand, while he held out his left to Sophy. Then, disengaging his right hand, he placed it upon hers, and bending down, kissed her cheek.

'What a long time you have been away!' exclaimed old Mr. Blake, as soon as the first greetings were over.   'We thought we should never see you again.'

'Well, here I am, and I don't intend to run away in a hurry.'

'How changed you are !   You look older, and you have let your beard grow longer.   I never approved of beards.   I think they give a man a coarse, common appearance.'

Hubert laughed, and busied himself in carrying various packages into the house, while Sophy glanced shyly at her cousin, at moments when she was not likely to meet his eye.

After dinner they all returned to the garden, and Hubert fetched a box which had just been opened.

'I've picked up a few little things I thought might interest you, while I was away,' he said ; and he proceeded to unpack his treasures and present them.

For his uncle there were several antiques, one or two rare coins, and a silver crucifix ; for Sophy two or three mosaics, some beauti-

ful bits of Venetian glass, and two brooches
—one a cameo, the other a piece of old-
fashioned workmanship in plain gold.

Sophy thanked him, but she felt disappointed. She had thought it likely that he
would bring her some little thing, and she had
unconsciously resolved that she would keep it
as long as she lived. These presents were too
fine, too valuable, and there were far too many
of them. She could not invest any one of
them with a special interest. If she did, it
would be her own selection, not his.

'And what have you been about, little one,
all this time?' he asked, laying his hand suddenly on Sophy's, as it lay on the garden-
table.

'Oh, nothing very remarkable,' she answered, quietly withdrawing her hand. 'We
went to the Academy, of course, and to the
Grosvenor—and to a Rose Show; and I have
been to one or two garden-parties.'

'We were thinking of going to the seaside
next week,' put in Mr. Blake; 'but we can't

find a house to suit us; and the drainage is always imperfect at these places—always. Some of those seaside resorts I consider nothing else than fever-traps. My wonder is that the people who stay there are alive.'

This was said with a judicial solemnity.

'If you had been in some of the towns I have visited, uncle, you would have had more cause for wondering. The drainage, I believe, was simply non-existent.'

Mr. Blake closed his eyes and shuddered.

Sophy rose to fetch something from the house.

'If there are any letters for me, Sophy, you might bring them along,' said Hubert.

Presently Sophy reappeared, bearing a tray on which was a pile of letters and newspapers. Hubert sprang up to relieve her of it.

'I had no idea there could be so many, or I wouldn't have troubled you,' he said, looking at the heap with an air of disgust.

Then he lit a cigar, and sat down again.

'Aren't you going to open your letters, Hubert?' said his uncle, after a pause.

'No; there's such a heap of them, and some are sure to be annoying. It will do quite as well to-morrow.'

'Some of them may be important,' rejoined the old man, after another pause.

Hubert saw that his laziness displeased the querulous old gentleman, so he began slowly to open his letters.

'I think the man should have been hanged,' he said between the puffs of his cigar, 'that invented penny stamps. I don't mean Sir Rowland Hill. It was another man—poor beggar, I forget even his name—who had the idea, and the man in office got all the glory and all the reward—*tulit alter honores.* As for Hill, he got a fortune and various ugly statues for an evil deed he never committed. Well, if these things are all to be set right one day, there's a good deal of clearing up to be done—that's all. What's this? A card for Lady Baldwin's garden-party—" thought

it possible you might be home in time ; hope
to have the pleasure of your company "—ah !
What one misses by going abroad !'

' Yes, indeed,' said the old gentleman ; ' and
I hope you won't leave this country again, so
long as I live. It may not be very long.'

' Then I should stay at home permanently,'
returned Hubert, knowing well enough that
none like better to be assured of a long life
than they who are fond of referring to their
approaching end.

' Another invitation, and another—a bill,
a circular, another circular. Some people
grumble at getting circulars ; I like them.
It's so pleasant to open a letter you expect to
have to answer, and find that you may drop it
at once into the basket with a clear conscience.'

' You don't encourage me to write to you
often,' said Sophy, with a little laugh.

' But he doesn't mean you, my dear,' said
the invalid.

' Mean Sophy ? Oh yes, particularly,'

said Hubert half absently, looking up from a letter he was reading.

Sophy knew, of course, that he was speaking ironically; but somehow she wished he had chosen to put the thing the other way.

'Well, you have one interesting correspondent, at any rate,' said Mr. Blake, who never could refrain from commenting upon the smallest actions of those near him.

Hubert made no reply. He was reading the letter a second time, while his cigar slowly went out. When he had finished it, he put his cigar into his mouth without noticing that it was unlighted, and sat silent, leaning his cheek on his hand. Sophy knew very well what letter he had been reading—at least, she knew the post-mark on it—and her heart beat faster as she bent her head over her work, and listened for Hubert's next words.

'I am afraid, sir,' he said at length, 'you will think me ungrateful for your kind welcome; but I think I must run off to-morrow

for a day or two. It's one of my Scotch
cousins,' he added apologetically, seeing a
look of grave displeasure on his uncle's face.
' He is in trouble of some sort, and he seems
to think I can be of use to him.'

' But that's no reason for your hurrying off
to Scotland before we have had time to look at
each other,' said the old gentleman peevishly.
' It's very unreasonable of him to expect such
a thing.'

'I think if I am to be of any use I must
go at once,' said the younger man, again unfolding Alec Lindsay's letter.

' If you are thinking of coming north after
your return to England,' ran the letter, ' I
wish you would come as soon as you can. I
feel as if a crisis in my life were approaching,
and as if I were all unprepared to meet it.
I need a friend at my side. My father has
set his heart on my becoming a Presbyterian
minister; and as I took my degree in May, he
thinks my next step will be to enter one of the
Free Church Colleges. I shall do nothing of

the kind; and I told him so as civilly as I could, but he seems to think he can break down my resolution. I believe he would be content if I were to take a place under Semple (you remember meeting him?) in my uncle's oil-works; but I am nearly as unwilling to do that as to don the Geneva gown. The worst of it is, my father's reproach that I don't know my own mind is true enough. And yet, I am sure I have no desire to lead an idle life. I wish you were here to advise me. Do you think I should have any chance at the English bar? Everybody says there is not the slightest opening at the Scotch bar; but I know so little of the world!'

'You do indeed, poor fellow!' was the reader's inward comment. But Hubert was deceiving himself when he ascribed his sudden resolution to set off for Scotland to a desire to see Alec Lindsay through his difficulties; or rather, he refused to listen to the whisper in which his heart told him that if he went to the Castle Farm he would in all probability find Margaret there. He had forced himself to stay away from Scotland for two years; he had come back to England (as he thought) cured of his passion; and at the first reasonable excuse the other half of his nature, the half which had so long been denied a hearing, sprang up and refused to be suppressed. 'At least go down to see her once more. You do not need to stay long, but to spend a day or two at the farm will hurt no one, and you may be of service to Alec.'

Thus spoke his heart while his judgment condemned; and Sophy, glancing at him, guessed something of what was going on in his mind. She had not failed to notice how her cousin (as she called him) had found his way down to Scotland again and again; and when she saw among his letters one bearing the Muirburn post-mark, she told herself that if he went to the north shortly after coming home she would know that her guess had been a right one. But she had not expected that before he had been four hours in the house he would have decided upon making the journey, and it was in a cold indifferent tone that she asked Hubert whether he thought of making an early start.

'If I take the 7.15 from Euston,' he replied, 'I can get to the farm the same evening. I had better do that; but don't make any alteration in your usual arrangements. I can easily get a cup of coffee at the railway station.'

When he came downstairs next morning, however, Sophy was tranquilly presiding over a well-furnished breakfast-table.

'Hullo!' he exclaimed; I really don't want anything. But how awfully good of you, Soph, to take so much trouble.'

'It's no trouble at all,' said she coldly, and with the faintest vestige of a smile. 'I very often get up at half-past five these summer mornings; and I'm glad of an excuse for having breakfast so early.'

They sat down together for a hurried meal, and Hubert began to talk in a more excited manner than was usual with him. Sophy, however, answered only by monosyllables.

'How is my uncle to-day?' he asked; 'oh! I forgot; you can't tell. I suppose he isn't awake yet. He seemed rather depressed last night.'

'Perhaps it was the reaction after the excitement of your coming home. And I think he was hurt at your leaving again so soon,' s e added.

She was angry at herself for having said this as soon as the words had left her lips; but Hubert did not seem to mind her.

'I'll be back in a day or two,' he said, without looking up.

Nothing more was said beyond the civilities of the table, till it was announced that the cab was at the door. Then Hubert started up in a fever to be gone.

'Good-bye, Sophy; you may look for me in — oh! I'll write, or wire, and let you know.'

'Good-bye, and a pleasant journey,' she

returned ; but she did not offer to go into the
hall to see him off.

Hubert   noticed   the   coldness   of   her
manner.

‘ Can I have offended her in any way ?’ he
said to himself.   ‘ Surely *she* is not such a
baby as to be annoyed at my leaving so soon.
I told them I had a reason.’

Meantime Sophy, standing well back from
the windows, watched her cousin get into his
hansom.   He looked back and waved his
hand, but there was no response.

‘ I fancy,’ he mused to himself as the cab
drove off—‘ I fancy girls in our rank of life
get stiffer and more conventional every year.
What harm would there have been, now, in
Sophy coming to the door to see me off ?   I
suppose it’s because she hasn’t a chaperon.
It’s a pity when people allow themselves to
be twisted out of shape by conventional rules.
Somehow, girls in the lower classes seem far
more natural, warmer hearted.   I wonder if
it is the fear of seeming improper that makes

Margaret so cold in her manner. If it were not for that, she would be perfect—simply perfect.'

And a series of dreams began, which lasted till the dreamer reached Euston Square.

Meantime Sophy, after fighting a successful battle with a rising flood of tears, set herself to begin, as patiently as she could, those important trifles which formed the occupation of her life.

CHAPTER XIV.

A TURNING-POINT.

THE hay-harvest was over, and the corn-harvest had not begun, so there was a comparatively 'slack time' at the farm. In a month, or less, every man and woman about the place, with probably two or three stray Irish labourers, would be busy with the sickle, or 'binding,' from early morning till late into the twilight; but for the present there was a period of repose.

Alec was sitting in the parlour with his father and sister. He had been at home, rather against his will, since the beginning of May. He was now a tall, broad-shouldered fellow, strikingly handsome in feature, but

rather awkward in limb—educated, so far as
a sufficiency of Latin, Greek, and mathe-
matics was concerned, but entirely ignorant of
modern languages and history, and almost as
ignorant of the world and human life as he
had been when he first went to College. His
winters had generally been spent in the society
of his friend Cameron (who had at last won
the desire of his heart, by being appointed
assistant to the Professor of Surgery), and
Cameron's influence upon him was stronger
than he had any idea of. In heart and
in experience Alec was still a boy, and he
was, boy like, letting his attention wander
from his volume of Spinoza to dream an
impossible dream, when he was recalled to
the earth by the sound of his father's voice.

'I met Mr. Dickson to-day, Alec.'

'Yes ?'

'He tells me the Presbytery meets next
week. Hadn't you better be getting ready
for the examination ? I suppose there is one
before you go to the Hall ?'

Alec was silent for a moment. He understood perfectly that the subject had been introduced in a half-indirect way, so as to throw upon him the burden of beginning the attack, as it were; and he understood, too, that the time had come for this question being settled.

'I thought I had told you, father, that I am not going to the Free Church Hall.'

'Margaret, will you leave us alone for a few minutes?' said Mr. Lindsay, and his daughter gathered up her work and left the room.

'So you have been deceiving us all this time?' said the laird in a low tone, fixing his cold, stern eyes upon his son.

'I have never deceived you!' burst out the young man hotly.

'When I agreed to furnish the means for your going to College,' said the laird slowly, 'I certainly understood that you were thinking of the ministry. What other reason was there for your staying here in idleness since you left College ? And why, in that case, did you go to College at all ? You have no wish to be a doctor, have you ? Answer me, sir !'

'No; I have not.'

'Then you *have* been deceiving me, I see.'

With a great effort Alec restrained himself.

'When I first went to Glasgow,' he began, 'I said I wanted to be educated. I said nothing of becoming a minister ; and I have never given you any reason to suppose that I intended doing anything of the kind.'

'You knew very well, sir, that it was not only my expectation, but my earnest desire, and that I never would have consented to throw away so much money on your education, merely to try to turn you into a fine gentleman.'

Alec flushed up, opened his lips, and closed them again without speaking. He could not tell his father that the insinuation conveyed by his words was untrue.

'Ah, Alec !' pursued the old man, in a softer tone, ' think what an opportunity you are throwing away! An opportunity that will never come again. What life could be higher or nobler than that spent in saving souls?' To this Alec made no reply. 'What are all the honours and wealth of the world compared to being the instrument of saving one soul?' asked Mr. Lindsay.

'But I have no call to the ministry,' said Alec at length.

'Have you sought for a call, my boy?' asked his father. 'Calls are not vouchsafed to those who do not listen for the summoning voice. Have you sought the guidance of God in this matter? Pray, my son, pray that you may be led aright. And now, tell Margaret and the servants to come to worship.'

Alec knew that his father meant to be kind —if only he would submit. He knew that the last words which the laird had spoken to him were sincere, but they grated upon him more unpleasantly than even the unjust and harsh things which his father had said at the beginning of the conversation. He resented this interference in the affairs of his own heart. He could see no rule or method of distinguishing between a Divine call and a suggestion of his own inclination. He was, in fact, out of harmony with the religious system in which he had been brought up. Sometimes he was willing to believe that the fault was entirely in himself; at other times he felt that the whole system was cold, hard, unlovely, and never free from a strong tendency to cant; but he was quite at a loss to know what he would have put in its place.

That evening Margaret contrived to see her brother alone before she went to bed. She came up to him in silence, took his hand in one of hers, and rested her other arm upon his shoulder.

'Alec,' she said, 'have you quite set your heart against being a minister?'

'That's not a fair way to put it, Maggie,' said he. 'Unless one's heart is naturally bent upon that calling, I don't think one should follow it.'

'But think of the good you might do!'

'Oh, that is such stuff, Maggie! Look at the ministers about here : what particular good do they do—Mr. Johnstone, or Mr. Fergus, or Mr. Simpson, or any of them ? On Saturdays they write (or don't write) their sermons. On Mondays, Tuesdays, Wednesdays, Thursdays, and Fridays they read, or potter about their gardens, or gossip with the neighbours.'

'They visit the sick,' put in Margaret.

'One afternoon a week is enough for that.'

' And they visit all their people regularly.'

' Yes ; and some of them simply pay calls, and the zealous ones give away tracts and ask how your soul is. A piece of impertinence!'

'Ah, Alec, you are sadly changed,' said Margaret, withdrawing her arm from her brother's shoulder.

' At any rate, I admit I am not fit to be a minister.'

' It will grieve father very much. He has set his heart upon it.'

' I can't help that. I can't do a thing like that—live a lie my whole life through—to please him.'

Margaret kissed her brother's cheek and left him. She had a feeling that he and she were far apart in religious matters, and she was right in her belief. Alec Lindsay had read modern philosophy; he had been taught at College that ' free-thought ' was a man's inalienable inheritance, and that it was a species of intellectual suicide to stifle a doubt. In the Calvinism he had learned in childhood there was plenty of dogma certainly; but then he did not like the dogma, and he saw no particular reason for believing it. He was, in fact, a Theist; but he gave his father no hint that his religious opinions had undergone a change. He knew very well that if he had so much as expressed a doubt as to the soundness of the Calvinist doctrine of Predestination, or the lawfulness of taking a walk or reading a novel on a Sunday, his father would have been shocked beyond expression, and would first have stormed at him, and then mourned him as one who had already sold himself to the Evil One.

Nothing more passed between father and son for some days, and then Mr. Lindsay asked Alec point-blank whether he was going to devote himself to 'the ministry of the Gospel.'

'No, father; I have no inclination of that kind, and I think that without a very strong disposition to such a life it would be wrong to begin it.'

The elder man fixed a cold look on his son, but made no reply.

'Don't you think I am right in saying so?' asked Alec.

The laird continued to gaze at his son without speaking, and Alec abruptly left the room.

About a week afterwards Alec was startled by his father saying to him one morning :

'I have just had a note from your uncle James. He is willing to take you into his office, and give you a small salary. The sooner you can get ready to go the better.'

'But I have no taste for a business life. I am not fitted for it, and I——'

'Perhaps you will tell me what you *are* fit for,' cried the old laird. 'Just understand this. If you choose to reject this offer, I shall have no more to say to you. You may take your own way, and I wash my hands of you. It seems to me you are bent on throwing away your chances.'

'Surely, sir, it is better to follow one's own inclination in choosing a profession ?'

'And what may be your inclination ?'

'I should like to be a lawyer.'

'And who is to support you while you are studying law ?'

'Others have begun as poor as I, and have risen to the top of the tree.'

'It is madness — sheer madness!' ex-claimed the laird, rising and pacing up and down the room.

'I can begin as clerk in an office,' said Alec.

'You shall do nothing of the kind!' shouted his father. 'You would know, if you knew anything at all about it, that you would not be paid while your articles were running. Perhaps you would like to be an advocate ?'*

Alec was silent ; for he knew that if he con-fessed that his real wish was to go to the bar, he would only the more effectually rouse his father's anger.

'Give me a week to think it over,' he said at length. 'It is not fair to ask me to decide a question that will influence the whole course of my life at a moment's notice.'

To this his father made no reply ; and Alec left the house, and wandered off to his old

* A barrister.

quarters at the ruined castle to hold counsel with himself.

At the end of an hour's thinking he had resolved to reject his uncle's offer. He saw quite plainly that if he accepted it he would be bound down for life to the narrow life of a Glasgow merchant—if, indeed, he had the chance of ever becoming more than an underling. He must give up the life of a student, for he knew that was practically incompatible with 'getting on in business.' And he must say good-bye to his ambitions. Rather than become a money-getting machine like one of the men he had met at his uncle's table, he would go back to teaching. Then, at least, he could keep up his reading, and continue to attend classes at College.

It was, no doubt, a foolish decision to make. But Alec could not help thinking that he could do better with himself than spend the next few years of his life as a clerk in his uncle's oil-works. He was determined to try to climb the ladder of Fortune, even if he should be thrown down and crushed under the feet of the crowd.

'After all,' he said to himself, as he rose from his seat and slowly made his way back to the farm—'after all, my life is my own. I can but try. I would rather make a struggle to rise, and fail, than not make the attempt. But I don't mean to fail. The question is, how can I get my foot on the first rung of the ladder? I haven't five pounds in the world.'

That was the difficulty; but next day a light was thrown on his path, and that from a quarter from which he had never expected it to come.

In the afternoon his cousin Semple turned up at the farm. This young man did not at all like the idea of his clever cousin coming to the oil-works. At present he was the only relative of Mr. James Lindsay in the place; and he thought it tolerably certain that at the old man's death the concern would pass into his hands. If another nephew were introduced, his own prospects might be seriously injured ; and so he had thought it worth while to run down to the farm, and see whether he could not secretly dissuade Alec from taking this step.

Of course he said nothing about the matter in the presence of Mr. Lindsay or Margaret ; and he could not help fancying that the keen eyes of the old laird were watching him as if to divine his intention. But when tea was over, the two young men strolled out together, and Semple began at once:

'So you are coming to us next week, I hear, Alec.'

'How do you know that ?' said the other, with inbred Scotch caution.

'Oh, Uncle James told me to expect you. Of course you know you'll have to begin at the beginning, and I fear you won't find it very much to your taste after your College life.'

'I may as well tell you, Semple, I've made up my mind not to go. But I'm " between the deil and the deep sea." I don't know what else I am to do.'

'What would you like to do?' asked Semple.

Secretly he was overjoyed at hearing of this resolution, and he determined to further it by every means in his power.

'What I would like to do would be to go to London, and enter the office of a good firm of solicitors. Between ourselves, Semple, I mean to go to the bar; but I can't begin to study in the regular way, because I've no money. I have heard that it's not a bad plan to go into a solicitor's office for awhile, to begin with, to learn the practice. But I know no one in London—no one in the profession, at least.'

'Perhaps I could help you there, Alec,' said the other, after a pause.

'I wish you could,' said Alec earnestly.

'Do you remember a fellow called Beattie? I think he was at College while you were there.'

'We didn't go to the same classes. He was two or three years in advance of me; but I remember his name very well. A clever fellow, wasn't he?'

'Plenty of brains, certainly,' answered Semple. 'Well, he had very much the same ideas as yourself. He went to London, and got into the office of a firm of solicitors —Hatchett, Small, and Hatchett; and now he is one of their managing clerks, though I believe he has never got his articles. Well, we are clients of Hatchetts'. They are carrying on a big lawsuit for us just now, and I dare say it will be a thousand pounds in their pocket. I should think they would oblige me in a thing of that sort; and Beattie, I know, will do what he can for you.'

'But the difficulty is, they wouldn't pay me any salary.'

'I should think they would give you something. You would very soon be of use to them. They paid Beattie, I know, almost from the first. But why don't you go straight to Uncle James, and ask him to give you something to start you in life ?'

Alec shook his head.

' I'll see if I can't manage that for you. He's a regular old screw. Five hundred pounds would be nothing to him.'

' It would make a considerable difference to me,' said Alec, with a laugh. ' You know, Semple, it's awfully good of you to trouble yourself about my affairs.'

' Oh no ; not at all.'

' Yes, it is. It's exceedingly kind of you. I shall never forget it as long as I live.'

Semple was rather amused than embarrassed by his cousin's expressions of gratitude.

' If he had tried his best, he couldn't have suited my book better,' said he to himself. ' But I must see what I can do with the old man.'

On reflection, however, he considered that it would be dangerous for him to approach Mr. James Lindsay himself. The shrewd old gentleman would be sure, he thought, to see through his motives. On his return to Glasgow, therefore, he betook himself to Miss Lindsay, and after telling her that Alec could not, and would not, go into 'the works,' he informed her of the plan that was on foot, and wound up by saying that Alec was such a clever fellow that it was a shame he should miss his chances for the sake of a little money. Surely his uncle would not grudge to do that much for him.

'It strikes me,' said the old lady, 'that the lad's best chance of making his fortune is to go into his uncle's office.'

She threw a keen glance at her visitor as she spoke, but Semple bore it unmoved.

'I dare say; indeed, I told him so, if I remember right. But he has made up his mind not to go.'

'Weel, if he gets the offer of the situation you speak o', I'll e'en do my best wi' Mr. Lindsay; but it winna be muckle, I doot.'

On this Semple took his leave, and that

night he went up to London, ostensibly on the affairs of the lawsuit. Beattie and he were old friends, and with his help he managed to convey to Mr. Hatchett the impression that Mr. James Lindsay would be grievously offended if they did not oblige him by taking his nephew into their office. It was all settled in half an hour; and next morning Semple was back in Glasgow.

All Miss Lindsay's eloquence, however, failed to make a deep impression on Uncle James. He would give the lad a hundred pounds, and that was all.

'The laddie's a fool,' said he, 'a clever fool; and that's aye the worst kind. If I were to give him mair, it wad a' come to the same thing in the end.'

Alec's father happened to be from home when the welcome letter arrived to tell him that the opening he had longed for had been found, and that the money difficulty had been removed. 'Don't say too much in thanking your uncle,' wrote Semple. 'There is nothing he hates like a fuss being made over his presents ; and, after all, there is no doubt you have a kind of claim upon him.'

This, however, was not the way in which Alec looked at the matter. Of course he went at once to see his uncle, and thank him, and his gratitude was so heartfelt that the old man was touched a little.

' Say nae mair, Alec ; say nae mair,' said he. ' I hope you'll do well, and do us credit ; and if there should be a positive necessity for it, I dare say another hunder might be forth-coming.'

' I trust it will not be necessary, uncle.'

' Weel, mony a man has won to the top o' the tree wi' less than a hunder pound in his pouch at the start. Guid-day !'

The difficulty which had seemed so in-surmountable had disappeared ; and to Alec it seemed as if the world lay at his feet. True, the parting with his father would be a painful one ; but that could not be helped. He would do his best to soften the old man's resentment at this second frustration of his wishes—and perhaps, he thought, some day his father would be glad that he had taken his own way, and determined to carve out his fortune with his own hand.

CHAPTER XV.

MR. LINDSAY listened in silence while his son detailed to him the plans he had made for his future; and when Alec came to an end, he made no remark.

'I hope, father, you do not disapprove of what I have done,' said Alec, after waiting for his father to speak.

'You are not acting in accordance with my wishes, as you know very well,' was the reply. 'I do not forbid your going to London, because you would pay no attention to me if I did. But I do not approve of your going. You will have no properly defined position in this firm of lawyers, of whom, after all, you know next to nothing. You are throwing away an excellent opportunity for a vague chance, out of mere caprice ; and you may live to regret that you have not taken my advice. I wish you would go over to Muirburn to-morrow, and tell Symes that I must have the new cart-wheels at once.'

Nor did Alec get much more sympathy from his sister ; though, unknown to him, she often dropped a tear over the articles of his outfit which she was busily preparing.

'You have never wished me good luck, Maggie,' he said on one occasion.

'You know I don't think you are doing right,' she answered without looking up.

'I am doing nothing wrong in choosing my own path in life,' cried Alec. 'And I must say,' he added, provoked at her want of sympathy, ' you and my father are not——' Then he stopped. 'But I'm not going to quarrel with you, this last week, Maggie.'

'I know quite well what you were going to

say, Alec. But I am very sorry you are going away at all, and the more so that you are going without my father's consent.'

Alec sighed impatiently.

'What *is* the use of going back to all that now ?' said he.

And his sister made no reply.

It may easily be imagined that it was a relief to Alec, and indeed to the whole family, when Hubert Blake made his appearance at the farm.

'Well,' he said, passing his arm through Alec's as they strolled together towards the river, 'so you have settled the great question without me ?'

'Yes.'

'I am sorry I am too late to be of any use ; but I came off as soon as I read your letter— that is, the very next morning. I think I had better go back to-morrow, for my uncle was not particularly well pleased at my running away directly after I got home.'

'I think it was more than good of you to

come,' answered the other; 'but now you are here, I do wish you could stay till I go, if you can. You see, things are not altogether smooth here, and——'

'All right. I will stay, and we can go up to London together. But what put it into your head to go into a lawyer's office?'

'I want to go to the bar, and this is the first step.'

'But why?'

'Because that is the great avenue by which men rise to political power. Three-fourths of the men in the House of Commons (that is, of the respectable men), who have not had the advantages of birth or fortune, have entered by that door.'

Blake stared at his companion.

'I had no idea you were so ambitious,' he said. 'But I doubt whether, even if you did get into the House, you would be much nearer your goal than you are now. And you have no idea of the difficulty of getting a practice at the bar, unless you have a connection among solicitors, or unless you are a born advocate.'

'Of course there will be plenty of difficulties. I've made up my mind to that. But I can see you think I ought to have taken my uncle's offer.'

'It might have been more prudent. If your ambition is to get into Parliament, you might have done that, perhaps, more easily as a wealthy manufacturer than as a struggling barrister. And yet, I don't know. Every man to his taste. It is a great thing to choose one's own work. You will have a wider and more varied life in London certainly, and—— there's somebody running after us.'

'It's Cameron!' cried Alec, as he turned round, and ran to meet his friend. 'This is awfully good of you, old fellow! coming to bid me good-bye,' he exclaimed, as he grasped his former chum by the hand.

'I heard you were going to the land of the southron, so I thought I would give the poor folk at the infirmary a holiday, and come to give you my blessing ere you departed,' answered the Highlander.

Alec introduced Blake to his old companion, and the three continued to stroll on in company.

'Don't you think,' said Cameron, addressing Blake, 'our friend here was greatly left to himself, when he decided not to help to illuminate the world by means of paraffin oil, and to woo the jade Fortune in your country instead ?'

'I don't believe you think he was wrong,' answered Blake, with a smile. 'You Scotchmen look upon England as your natural prey.'

'It's not everyone that goes to fish that comes back wi' a full creel,' responded Cameron ; 'but we'll hope that Lindsay will spoil the Egyptians of much fine gold, and rise to be Lord Chancellor. Last summer I took a run down to Manchester, and as the assizes were going on, I looked in at the courts. It was a fearfu' sight.'

'Was it a murder case ?' asked Blake.

'No; I mean the scores o' young an' middle-aged men daunderin' about in wigs and gowns, with their hands in their pockets. I suppose every one of them thought he had a prospect of being Lord Chancellor. One of them was a man I had met at College—you may remember him, Alec; Ferguson is his name. He asked me to dine at their mess, and after dinner they sang a song about that. I mind the chorus. It went something like this,' and Cameron sang in a deep bass voice:

> 'Then drink, brothers, drink,
>   And let every brother drink,
> Who has ever held a soup* prosecution ;
>   For it's possible he may
>   Be Lord Chancellor some day—
> If he's only got a sound constitution.'

'Tell us where you have been, Blake, since I saw you last,' said Alec, anxious to turn the conversation from himself and his own prospects.

'Oh, the usual round—Switzerland, Rome,

---

* So called, because the unimportant prosecutions at some Quarter Sessions are handed round to the junior members of the bar, one to each, like so many plates of soup.

and Venice. I spent a good while in Venice.'

Cameron looked at the Englishman with admiration and envy.

' I would like fine to see Rome,' he said to himself in an undertone. Then he began to ask questions about those cities, which Blake answered as well as he was able.

After a time the conversation changed again, for Alec began to talk to Cameron about their old College friends, and Blake walked on in silence. He was comparing, in his own mind, his lot in life with that of the two young men beside him. His advantages had been so much greater than theirs, and his performances had been so trifling ! He had seen, and admired, and copied : they had struggled and acted. He was already feeling wearied of life, while Cameron was beginning what promised to be a successful career of great usefulness, and Alec was bravely setting out to battle with the world. Would he never be able to give anything to his fellow-men in return for the food he ate—never be able to do anything on which he could afterwards look back with satisfaction ?

Alec interrupted these reflections by hinting that they had better return to the farm, as it was getting late, and it would soon be time for supper.

Cameron was in capital spirits, and he managed to infect the whole party with his genial humour. Even Mr. Lindsay thawed visibly, and spoke to his son more kindly than he had done since Alec had refused to walk in the way he had chosen for him.

The next two days passed rapidly and pleasantly, Cameron still remaining a guest at the farm. Blake, meanwhile, perceived quite clearly that time had made no change in his sentiments towards Margaret. She seemed to him more beautiful than ever, and more soft and womanly than she had appeared before. And in spite of his better judgment, he longed to end the struggle that was going on within him, by asking her to be his wife.

22—2

It was the afternoon of the third day, Alec's last day at home; and the four young people were sitting out of doors. Margaret was sewing something for her brother; Alec and Cameron were stretched on the grass, playing a game of chess. Blake was glancing over a newspaper, when, happening to look up, he saw Cameron looking at Margaret's downcast face with such a tender, admiring gaze, that he dropped his eyes immediately, while a strange thrill passed through his heart. Cameron had no idea that he had been observed, for Alec's eyes were fastened on the chess-board, while Blake was sitting in the background, apparently intent on his newspaper.

'Check!' cried Alec; and Cameron bent once more over the board.

Blake rose, and walked slowly away, across the empty stackyard. So he was not alone in his admiration of Margaret! Was he content that another should woo and win her? Passionately he told himself that he was not content. He wandered on for some minutes, not thinking where he was going, and after making a circuit returned to the farm.

Suddenly he came upon Margaret, sitting on a bench which overlooked the little flower-garden.

He sat down beside her, and was surprised to see that her eyes were filled with tears. She was the first to speak.

'Mr. Blake,' she said, 'I wish to ask a great favour from you. I wish you to keep a watch over my brother in London. He will be quite among strangers; and he has seen very little of the world. I should think he might easily be led astray. Will you see him when you can, and do your best to warn him if he is in danger, to keep him from bad companions, and to encourage him when he is cast down, as I am sure he often will be ?'

Her beautiful eyes, still laden with tears, were turned upon her companion.

'I will, indeed,' said Blake, 'for your sake, as well as for his own.'

'Thank you,' said Margaret simply.

'But I wish,' he continued in a low voice, hardly conscious of what he said—'I wish you would give me a better right to look after him—the right of a brother.'

She looked up hastily, not understanding his meaning. His face made it plain to her.

'Dear Margaret,' he began, gently laying hold of her hand.

But she started to her feet.

'No, no, Mr. Blake,' she said, almost in a whisper. 'That can never be.'

'Never, Margaret? Why not? Why should you turn from me? You know me well, and I hope, at least, you don't dislike me. If you can but learn to love me, how happy you would make me!'

'No,' she answered; 'I don't think I could make you happy. Your life has not been like mine. My ways, my thoughts are not like yours. You have tastes and habits which—oh, it is quite impossible !'

'All that goes for nothing, Margaret. Tastes and habits are soon acquired. You would soon learn to love the world of art, the wider world I could lead you into ;' and again he tried to take her hand.

But again she drew it away.

'I know I could make you happy,' said Hubert.

'But, Mr. Blake,' she said in a low voice, ' you are not a Christian.'

Hubert was silent. From a man he would have resented the imputation. Yet he knew that, in Margaret's sense of the word, she only spoke the truth.

'Not as you are, perhaps,' he said at length ; 'but that need not part us. You will make me a Christian ; you will teach me.'

Margaret shook her head sadly, and turned away.

'Don't go yet,' cried Hubert, following her.

'Answer me one question first. Do you love me? That is the only thing I care for.'

'It is not the only thing,' answered the girl. 'I would never marry a man who was not a Christian.'

Hubert saw it was useless to argue.

'Do you love me?' he repeated.

Margaret looked up, her lovely face pale with emotion.

'No,' she answered.

'Will you not try to love me?'

'No, I cannot,' she repeated in a lower tone.

'Do, Margaret.'

'No; please don't ask me again.'

Her tone was firmer and clearer now, and Hubert saw that the case was decided.

'If I come again—in six months, or a year?'

'You would only distress me. I should only tell you again what I tell you to-night.'

'Is that your final answer, Margaret?'

' It is—my final answer.'

' Then—good-bye. I will not forget my promise about your brother.'

He turned his back on the farm, and walked away by himself, not returning until it was time for the evening meal. He felt the disappointment keenly, all the more keenly that he had never anticipated a refusal. It was cruel to think that Margaret was sacrificing his happiness, and perhaps her own, to what he called her fanaticism. He was furious to think that she would never be his, that he might entreat her to the end of time, and she would never yield.

As for Margaret, she slipped into the house and was very little seen again that evening. No one ever knew what had passed between her and Hubert Blake. Not even to her own heart did Margaret answer the last question which he had pressed upon her.

That night she waited long behind the half-open door of her room, that she might waylay her brother as he came upstairs. At last the lights were put out, and she heard his footstep.

She came up to him with a half-articulate whisper, and threw her arms round his neck. Then she sobbed, as if her heart would break.

'Don't, Maggie. Don't, dear old Maggie,' whispered her brother as he kissed her.

'Oh, Alec! you are going away. Perhaps I may never see you again ; and I've been so cold and unkind ! Oh, Alec, I don't want to lose you : that was the reason of it. But I am so sorry ! I would give anything—all I have in the world—if only I had behaved differently.'

'It was my fault, Maggie, every bit as much as yours.'

'No ; no ; no !'

'Yes, it was. But never mind. What does it matter now ? I know you love me, Maggie, and that's all I care for.'

'And you will write to me ?'

'Every week, Maggie.'

'Whether you have anything to say or not?'

'Whether I have anything to say or not. And I will come to see you at Christmas.'

'*Will* you?'

'I will, though it should only be for a day.'

'Then I shall have something to look forward to. Oh, Alec, how good you are!'

And an hour passed before the brother and sister parted.

Next morning the good-byes were said in haste, but they were not so painful as Alec had anticipated. His father's reserve broke down at the last; he embraced his son, and put an envelope into his hand containing fifty pounds in bank-notes.

'Take it, lad,' he said, as Alec would have put it back in his hand—'take it; I can easily spare it. It's hard to part with you; and I had hoped—but never mind that now. Fear God, Alec, and keep His command-ments, for that is the whole duty of man.'

' Oh, father !' cried Alec ; ' I almost wish
—if I had known——'

' Come, my boy ; it's time you were gone.
You will miss the coach.'

Another hurried embrace from Maggie,
another shake of the hand from his father,
and he was gone ; and the father and
daughter went back together to the silent
and empty house.

CHAPTER XVI.

IN LONDON.

Who has not tried to put into words his first impressions of London ? And who has not failed ? Probably, if people were quite careful not to impose upon themselves, they would feel bound to confess that, after the first feeling of bewilderment was over, their chief impression was one of a vague disappointment. They knew that they had set foot in the Metropolis of the Empire, and they could not help forgetting that London is not to be seen in half an hour.

This, at least, was Alec Lindsay's experience. When he emerged from the railway-station and found himself in the Euston Road, he could hardly believe that he had at last reached the city of his dreams. With his overcoat over his arm and his bag in his hand (avoiding, like a thrifty Scot, the needless expense of a cab), he trudged slowly eastwards, taking mental notes as he went. He was surprised at the comparative stillness around him. He had often heard of the bustle in the streets of London; but the Euston Road was quieter than many a street in Glasgow. Then the houses offended him. They were much lower in height than those to which he had been accustomed, and much uglier. He gazed with contempt on the tumble-down buildings of wood, or of brick not much more durable than wood, projected from the houses to the pavement. He was surprised at the absence of hurry, at the street children playing about (as much wrapped up in their play as if they had been on a village-green), at the half-intelligible Cockney dialect.

After reaching King's Cross Alec made his

way to a small street lying to the north of Gray's Inn, where there was a private boarding-house, and there he established himself till he should find suitable lodgings. As soon as he had had a cup of tea he sallied out again into the streets; for the roar of London was in his ears, and he could not keep still.

'I wish Cameron were going to hunt for diggings with me,' he said to himself, as his mind flew back to the time when his friend had compelled Mrs. Macpherson to admit him to her house.

Then suddenly the sense of loneliness descended upon him, almost like a tangible thing. He was standing at the crossing, close to the Metropolitan Railway Station, where the crowd was thickest. Half mechanically he noted one and another come and go, and vanish in the crowd, like autumn leaves on a swollen river. They came and went, and he was alone. In this great swarm of human creatures none knew his face, not one knew even his name.

The air was thick and tainted, heavy with a thousand offensive odours ; and the yellow sunshine from the sinking sun seemed to be struggling in vain to teach the dwellers in this unlovely city something of the peace and beauty in the great world beyond. And Alec, looking up, saw its radiance. He saw the rose-colour in the air. He saw a few unconsidered dirty panes of glass, high up in the gable of a warehouse, flashing like gems on the wall of the city that hath no need of the sun—and he remembered that the same sunlight was lighting up the wide moors and the bare slopes of Ben Ime, and playing on the green seaweed and the gray rocks, where none but angel-eyes were looking on.

Afterwards Alec came to know London well, for he was never tired of wandering about the streets. He came to know that Cheapside and the Strand were not ' London,' nor even Westminster or Piccadilly. He lost himself, over and over again, in labyrinths of small, grimy streets, each twenty feet of which made a separate home. He found that in the East End there were miles and miles of land covered with manufactories, warehouses, and houses of repulsive ugliness filled with hard-working people. He came to the conclusion at last that the one thing in which London was unique was its unsearchableness. In other towns there were half a dozen, perhaps a dozen, important thoroughfares ; here they were numberless. And no sooner had he studied one neighbourhood till he knew it very well, than he found another inhabited by people who had totally different habits and modes of life, different interests ; speaking, perhaps, a different language.

On the morning after his arrival Alec presented himself at the office of Messrs. Hatchett, Small, and Hatchett, in Theobald's Road. He was shown into a large, well-furnished, but not very clean room, lined with calf-covered volumes, which were kept more for show than for use. Here, early as it was, the senior partner was seated, busy over his correspondence. He looked up as Alec entered, showing a face which expressed less than any human countenance which Alec had ever beheld. It was the face of a man who had trained himself to say the correct thing, and not a word more—who had schooled himself for thirty years to allow nothing of such feelings or sentiments as he might possess to appear in his face. His hair was well brushed; his coat fitted perfectly; his boots were all that boots could be; his tie was of exactly the proper hue, neither sombre nor brilliant; his manner—to those whom he considered his equals—was unexceptionable.

'So you are Mr. Lindsay—eh? Glad to see you. Take a seat. A connection of a client of ours in Scotland, I believe. A nephew? Yes—just so——'

(Dictating to a clerk at his side:)

'Butler and Smith, solicitors. Dear Sirs,— We beg to acknowledge your letter of yesterday's date. Your offer of £300 and costs is quite inadequate. We have briefed Mr. Bussel, and the case will come on for hearing, we expect, in three days' time. Yours, etc.——Major-General Potts. Dear Sir,—Yourself *v.* Brown. The defendant has offered £300 and costs, which is more than we expected, and we advise you to accept it. The costs, of course, are very heavy; and in the event of an adverse verdict they would fall entirely upon you. We are, dear sir, yours faithfully.——By the way, Mr. Tibbets, see that that brief in Brown and Potts' case goes over to Mr. Bussel this forenoon.—And now, Mr. Lindsay, what can I do for you ? You want to see a little of our business, try what it is like before taking articles, I believe ?'

As he spoke, Mr. Hatchett opened another envelope, glanced over its contents, and placed them on a little heap of papers at one side of the table.

'I am not sure yet that I shall take articles,' said Alec. 'It is very probable I may not do so.'

'We never take pupils,' said Mr. Hatchett,

his eyes on a fresh letter as he spoke. 'It is our invariable rule. But we have no objection to your being here a few months, to oblige Mr. Lindsay—none at all.'

Then he seemed to forget all about the new clerk and his affairs, and remained plunged in thought for some seconds. Finally, he laid aside the letter without speaking, and went on to open another.

Before him was a pile of letters which had yet to be got through ; and on one side lay a bundle of deeds and documents which had just come up from the law-stationer. At his right hand stood two baskets, one being a deep one for the envelopes and waste paper, the other a shallow one for the letters themselves. On a table was a tray for the documents which came by the post.

Before Mr. Hatchett had finished his correspondence the door opened, and a tall, thin young man, with a pale face, black hair, large features, and a keen, shrewd expression of countenance, came into the room.

'Ah! Mr. Beattie—a little late, eh ?'—and the lawyer began to discuss with his manager in a low tone the details of the business before them. It was not until that was over that Alec's existence was remembered. Then his fellow-countryman came up with a smile and shook hands with him.

'Yes; I think you had better take charge of Mr. Lindsay for the present,' said Mr. Hatchett. 'I dare say you will be able to make him useful. And as to that mortgage of the Waste Paper Utilization Company, you had better write at once and refuse their offer. That's all, I think.'

Alec followed his new acquaintance up two flights of stairs into a small room crowded with tables, every one of which was covered with bundles of papers.

'This is my den,' said Beattie, 'but I thought you would like a room to yourself, so I told them to clear out a little place for you across the passage ;' and he led the way to another room on the same floor.

It was small, dusty, and, what was even worse, dark, as a tall building opposite the only window obscured the light. There was no carpet on the floor. In one corner stood an old bookcase with cupboards underneath for papers; and in another there was a dilapidated fireplace.

'Sorry to put you into such a poor place, but perhaps we'll be able to get you a better room by-and-by,' said Beattie with a smile; and Alec assured him that he wanted nothing better.

' What sort of work would you like to begin with ?' asked the managing clerk, with another smile. ' Conveyancing ? or common law ? or chancery practice ?'

' Really, I don't know. Whatever department I can be of most use in. I shall have to learn something of all of them, I suppose.'

' Conveyancing is my own branch,' said Beattie. ' Suppose you begin with that.'

He left the room, and soon returned with an armful of deeds and papers.

'This,' he said, touching a blue paper, 'is an abstract of that deed. Compare it with the deed, and you will see how it is done. Then copy it on these large sheets. Here is one you may use as a model. And then you may try to draw an abstract of this deed,' and he touched another one as he spoke, 'in exactly the same way. If you are not sure of anything, come and ask me;' and, with another smile, Mr. Beattie left the room.

Alec could not help admiring the clearness and precision with which the directions were given. He found the work interesting from its novelty, and by no means difficult.

He had been busy for an hour or two, when the door slowly opened, and a shabbily-dressed little man with red hair sidled into the room, and, hardly looking at its occupant, began to hunt for a volume among the book-shelves.

Alec merely glanced up, and bent again over his work. When he looked up a second time, the little man was standing with a book in his hand, pretending to consult it, but evidently using it as a pretext for taking stock of the new clerk.

' Good-morning,' said Alec.

' Guid-day to ye, Mr. Lindsay,' replied the other, extending a not very clean hand across the table. ' I'm glad tae see ye. It's a pleasure to see ony ane frae the auld country.'

' You're in the office, I suppose,' said Alec.

The other nodded, put his hands in his trousers-pockets, and stared at Alec from the other side of the table.

His appearance was certainly not prepossessing. His hair was long and untidy, his eyes bloodshot and shifty; and his chin was covered with an ill-shaved beard. He was evidently not a young man, but he had the manners of an ill-bred boy. His expression was a mixture of shrewdness, meanness, and presumption. Alec wanted to get rid of him, but he hardly knew how to do it.

'You're from Glasgow?' said the red-haired man.

'Yes.'

'And I'm from the Mearns. That's no far from Glasgow. I used to ken the place weel. My name's MacGowan. Ye've maybe heard o' my uncle, Dr. MacGowan of Strathbogie?'

'Not that I remember;' and Alec turned again to his papers.

But the other took no notice of that.

'An' to think that you were in Glasgow but yesterday!' exclaimed MacGowan.

'Is it long since you came to London?' asked Alec, by way of being civil.

'Fifteen years; fifteen weary years, come Martinmas,' answered MacGowan with an emphatic nod. 'And, though I ken mair o' what they ca' law—though it's a poor thing compared wi' Scottish Jurisprudence—than either Mr. Hatchett, Mr. Small, or Mr. Beattie—and that's no sayin' muckle—I'm just where I was fifteen years ago, a clerk, wi' thirty-five shillin's a week.'

Alec murmured something by way of sympathy, and the other went on :

'Paid monthly, Mr. Lindsay, paid monthly. And it's sometimes very inconvenient to wait till the first o' the month for the sma' monthly steepend.'

Alec murmured something still more indistinct.

'And the cashier here has a heart like the nether mill-stone. Precious little o' the milk o' human kindness in *his* carcass. He'd see ye driven oot to dee on the street—he'd see a man wantin' his denner, before he'd advance him a poor five shillings on his next month's screw. An' that minds me, Mr. Lindsay. Next Wednesday is the first o' the month. If you could lend me a sma' sum till that time—say five shillings.—Thank ye, sir. I look upon you as a true Scotchman, who will not see a brother Scot in extremities without extending the helping hand.'

He stopped suddenly, and had barely time to pocket the coins when the door opened, and Beattie came into the room. At the sight of his cold, impassive face, MacGowan shrank back, and turned in confusion to the bookcase. Beattie fixed him with his eye ; and MacGowan, not daring to meet it, slipped past his superior into the passage.

'An idle, drunken, good-for-nothing vagabond,' said Beattie, as soon as he had disappeared. 'I advise you not to speak to him. He will take all sorts of liberties with you if you allow him.'

'Then he looked over the abstracts, explained one or two points, and ended by asking Alec to dine with him that evening at the Holborn Restaurant.

Of course Alec accepted the invitation ; but he did so without any feeling of pleasure. Beattie had been civil, and even friendly ; but somehow Alec could not bring himself to like him. He smiled too often, and his smile was a purely conventional one, from the teeth outwards, fading away in a moment and leaving his face as stern and cold as before.

His features were harsh, and his long upper lip gave an unpleasant look to his face. But most of all Alec disliked his accent. It smacked strongly of affectation. The Scotch intonation was still there and refused to be effaced, while the English manner of speaking had evidently been laboriously grafted upon the original stock. The result was not satisfactory to anyone but Mr. Beattie himself.

Soon after Alec and his host had taken their seats at table that evening, Mr. Beattie elicited the fact that Mr. James Semple was virtually at the head of his uncle's oil-works, and that in all probability he would be the old man's heir; and from that moment Alec became a very secondary person in his eyes. The two had not much in common, and the conversation languished till it seemed at one point as if it would die out altogether. As the evening proceeded, however, and the wine in the bottles diminished, matters improved; and by the time the two young men had lit their cigars, Beattie was giving his views on the state of society and the general scheme of things with considerable freedom.

'There's no place in the world,' said he, with much emphasis, 'where there's so many beggars on horseback, as there are in and about this city of London. Go out on the streets, or go to any of the fashionable suburbs, and see the kind of people who roll past in their carriages. If you were to take the master out, put on his coachman's livery, and set him on the box, put his overcoat and hat on the coachman and get *him* inside, no one would notice the difference.'

'But there is the aristocracy.'

'True; but it is the rich parvenus, the nobodies, that make London. And, after all, I fancy a long purse and a lavish hand will win a man's way into any house in this country. Look at Baron Brand, as he calls himself! I remember when that man came to our office ready to do any dirty work we liked to put him to. And see where he is now.'

'But there are surely circles of men of letters, of artists,' began Alec.

'No doubt; but who knows or cares anything about them? They might be swept off the face of the earth to-morrow, and London would never miss them.'

It occurred to Alec that the same thing might be said of a good many other social institutions in London, but he held his tongue.

'Wealth is the great power, after all,' resumed Beattie, 'even in politics. Name ten famous men in the country who are not rich, or at least rich enough to live as wealthy people do. You can't.'

'There's Ruskin.'

'Ruskin was rich, rich enough, at least, to travel and spend his time as he liked, or he never could have become famous. Years ago, with diligence and some ability, a man could push his way to the front. But the crowd is too thick for that now.'

'But, surely, eminence in one's profession——'

' Ay, but how is that attained ?'

' By learning it thoroughly, and——'

Beattie burst into a hoarse laugh.

' My dear fellow, you have the simplest notions. Never mind ; you'll know better in time. Learning ! Now, look here. Take our own profession. That little drunken beggar in our office, MacGowan, knows more law than most men with wigs on their heads I have come across—more than many a Q.C. I dare say he told you as much himself.'

' He did,' said Alec, with a laugh.

' And he gets eighty or ninety pounds a year. Take my own case. I know as much, and am as good a man of business (though I say it myself) as any of my governors. They give me three hundred a year, while young Hatchett has as many thousands. And what then ? His tailor has more than twice as much as he has. I know it for a fact.'

' I never thought it mattered very much what a man has.' said Alec serenely.

Beattie looked at him curiously, and went on :

'You are ambitious, then ?   And you think learning, diligence, and so on, will help you up the ladder ?'

'That's what I mean to try,' said Alec with a laugh, and something of a blush.

'It is impossible, or next to it.   How many men, able men, well-educated men, do you think there are in London, grinding away at law, or writing books, or painting pictures, or designing buildings till their hair is gray ? Who ever hears of them, or thinks of them ? They will never reach even the first rung of the ladder.   Never.'

'How, then, do men get on ?'

Beattie lifted his eyebrows.

'Some, a few, have exceptional gifts, and when they do get a chance they let it be seen. But, as a rule, those who come to the front don't push their way through the crowd ; they climb over other men's heads.   They hang on to what men they do know, and flatter or bother them into giving them the opportunity they want. Then, when they have got it, they make the most of it. They never lose a chance of advertising themselves. Better, they say, be spoken of as a cad or a fool, than not be spoken of at all. They never lose an opportunity of sticking a spoke in a rival's wheel ; and they will half ruin a man one minute, and meet him with a "Well, old man," the next, as if they were the greatest friends in the world.'

Alec's face wore an expression of deep disgust.

'And the beggars on horseback, having filled their purses out of some tobacco-shop, or grog-shop, or shoddy-shop, put their thumbs in the arm-holes of their waistcoats, lean back in their carriages, and think themselves the pick of mankind, till a lord comes their way, and then they bow down in the dust before him—that is, if he's richer than they are.'

Alec was getting a little tired of his friend's cynicism, so he rose to go.

'I don't believe it,' said he to himself, as he made his way home. 'There are plenty of fellows, fellows who have got on too, who wouldn't do a dirty thing to save their lives. If it is impossible—well, so be it.'

William Beattie was soured by disappointment. He would not allow for the natural advantages which those before him in the race derived from wealth and business connections. He hated his employers, because they showed no disposition to 'give him his articles,' and make him a member of the firm. He greatly longed to throw up his post and try to find a nearer road to wealth, but this he did not dare to do. As for his sneers at 'beggars on horseback,' they were simply due to envy.

CHAPTER XVII.

AN UNCONVENTIONAL GUEST.

WHEN Hubert Blake returned to Highgate after his hurried journey to Scotland, it was evident to Sophy's eyes that something had happened to him. Before he went north he was bright and full of spirits. Now he was listless, moody, and unsociable. If he had been his own master, he would not have gone back to London at all. He would have set off at once for another long, aimless tour. But he felt that something was due to his uncle, and shortly after he left the Castle Farm, he made his appearance without warning at Grove House.

'Why didn't you write and say you were

24—2

coming ?' asked old Mr. Blake, in his usual peevish tone.

'Really, sir, I didn't think of it.   I didn't suppose it mattered.'

'One always likes to know when anything is going to happen,' said the old man, half offended at his nephew's want of courtesy.

And Hubert, totally unconscious that he had given any offence, sauntered out into the garden.   Sophy was there, sitting on her favourite garden-seat, and as Hubert came forward she rose to meet him, with a smile on her face.

'Well, Sophy,' was his greeting, as he sat down beside her, ' how have you been getting on ?'

'Exactly as usual.   And you ?'

'Oh, I ?   Well ; I found that the matter I went to Scotland about had got settled without my intervention, as things have a habit of doing if you only let them alone. So I stayed a few days at the farm ; and then I came back.   That's all.'

'You might have told us you were coming.'

'So my uncle said to me. Perhaps it would have been more polite; but what's the use of making a fuss? My coming or going isn't a thing of so much importance.'

After that nothing was said for a minute or two; and Hubert, stooping down, picked up a few pebbles, and began jerking them with his thumb into the laurels.

'Have you come back to town for the winter?' asked Sophy at length.

'I don't know,' said the other absently.

Sophy stole a glance at her companion.

'I don't think uncle will be able to make up his mind to go away at all this autumn. I think it such a pity.'

To this Blake made no reply; he only went on pelting the bushes.

'The Colmans called here yesterday,' began Sophy once more. 'They came to tell us that Edmund Colman has taken a first-class.'

'Most awful prig!' murmured Hubert under his breath.

'I am going to have three hundred snow-drop bulbs set in the grass-borders in October.' said Sophy, changing the subject. 'Don't you think they will look very nice?'

'I dare say.'

Sophy said no more; and Hubert got up to return to the house. As he looked round before moving away, he was struck by the expression on Sophy's face, as she bent over her work, and he sat down again.

'What's the matter, Sophy? Have I offended you in any way?'

'No.'

'Is it because I didn't write to say I was coming. 'Surely——'

'Oh no; not at all.'

'There is something. Don't let us have a misunderstanding, for Heaven's sake. If I have hurt you, tell me frankly what it is.'

'It is only this,' said Sophy, gathering courage, 'that our old relations seem to have changed entirely. Before you went away you used to be interested in our little doings. Now you don't care at all. We don't seem to belong to the same family now. You tell us nothing about yourself. You go away for two years, and——'

Sophy stopped suddenly.

'Oh, dear me!' Hubert groaned within himself; but when he spoke his tone was kind and gentle.

'The fact is, Sophy, I'm spoiled for want of something to do. It would do me all the good in the world to be forced to earn my bread as a day-labourer for twelve months. But I haven't the pluck to do it.'

'You have your profession,' said Sophy.

'I'm sick of it. Everything seems so dull and tasteless, as if nothing were really worth anything. I'm tired of my life—tired of myself, I suppose, that is. Do you never feel like that?'

Sophy sighed inaudibly, and made no reply.

'I've a great mind to put twenty pounds in my pocket, go to New York, and try to make a living there somehow. I suppose I'd fail: and I don't see that it would very much matter. Nothing does matter very much, does it?'

'Not if one lives for one's self,' said Sophy.

She feared she had said too much, but her companion did not seem to notice it.

'By the way,' he said after a pause, 'that young cousin you've heard me speak of, Alec Lindsay, has just come up to town. I ought to be civil to him. He's not a bad sort of fellow—a little countrified, that's all. He gives one the feeling of there being a good deal in him, that will come out some day. Do you mind my asking my uncle if I may invite him to come here and dine some evening?'

'Of course I don't mind. I shall be very pleased to see him.'

'I'm afraid you won't find him amusing. He's very simple and outspoken. In fact, he

is one of those fellows who don't need to be
outspoken. His face always tells you what
he is thinking of before he opens his lips.'

At this point a servant came in and
intimated that Mr. Blake was tired of his
own company, and Hubert and Sophy went
into the house together.

Some days passed before Blake could
procure Alec's address by means of a letter
to the farm ; and then he asked his Scotch
cousin to dinner.

It was a new experience for Alec. Everything at Grove House seemed daintier, more
delicate, and more precise than what he had
been accustomed to. Never in his life had
he seen so much money and trouble lavished
upon the petty details of existence ; never
had he seen the art of comfortable living
carried to such perfection.

When the little party adjourned to the
drawing-room after dinner, this impression
was strengthened. The soft low seats, the
thick carpet — for Mr. Blake would not

tolerate stained boards and Eastern mats—
the softly shaded and tinted lights, the
delicate china, all helped to produce the
effect. The young Scotchman felt too big,
too strong and awkward, for these luxurious
surroundings.

Sophy could scarcely tell what to make of
her guest. She liked him; she liked his
frank, open face, and his unconventional, un-
affected manners; she liked his strong northern
speech. But she hardly knew how to talk to
him. He had no idea of the art of saying
little polite nothings for the sake of keeping
conversation going.

'You have only come south lately?' she
asked, with a smile.

'Only ten days ago.'

'And how do you like London?'

'What do you mean by London?'

Sophy was naturally at a loss for an answer,
and Alec went on:

'London means so many things. The
houses are very mean-looking.'

'But the people?' asked Sophy, hiding her amusement under a conventional smile. 'How do you like them?'

'They are very smart,' answered Alec, speaking with great deliberation, 'and quick in all they do, and selfish, and always in a hurry; and they think that London is all the world.'

'You have seen some of the sights, I suppose?'

'Yes. I went to the National Gallery to see the pictures. Some of them I couldn't make anything of. But some of them were simply splendid. And Westminster Abbey! I never saw anything like it!'

'You admired the Abbey, then?'

'It is—oh! I can't find words to tell you what I thought of it! It provoked me so, to see the stupid people going about with their faces as calm as if they were going to dinner, or staring at one lump of a monument after another. It seems as if it were alive, and knew how beautiful it is. The columns seem never tired of springing up, and up, and up, as if they would reach to heaven; and yet they are satisfied when they join each other in a perfect arch. Who built it? Who imagined it?'

'I'm sure I don't know, Mr. Lindsay,' said Sophy, glancing to Hubert for information. He had been watching Sophy, amused by her wonder at the boy's enthusiasm.

'It was built by the Benedictines, I believe,' said he.

'I thought nothing could be finer than Glasgow Cathedral till I saw Westminster,' said Alec simply.

'Have you a cathedral at Glasgow? I thought you were all Presbyterians in Scotland,' said Sophy.

'Oh, a very fine one,' said Hubert, answering for his cousin — 'small, but a good specimen of its era. And the crypt is particularly good, the finest in Britain, I believe.' (This gratified Alec immensely.) 'And what did you think of St. Paul's? You have seen St. Paul's, I suppose?'

' I liked the outside ; at least, it seems very grand. And when I first went under the dome I felt as if I had been on the top of a mountain.'

' When you went to the top of the dome, the stone gallery, I suppose you mean,' said Sophy.

' No ; when I went under the dome.'

' I understand you,' said Hubert. ' It gives you something of the same sense of space and vastness.'

' But there's very little beauty about it,' continued Alec. ' It's big, and that is about all. It's nothing to be compared with Westminster.'

' Will you give us some music, Sophy ?' asked Hubert, moving towards the piano.

Sophy could play well—she had plenty of time for practice — and she chose one of Beethoven's sonatas.

' Do you like that ?' she asked at the end of the first movement, turning to Alec.

He shook his head.

'I dare say it's very beautiful, but I don't understand what it means in the least. I don't care for it.'

'Frank, at least,' murmured Sophy to herself, as she turned over the leaves of her music-book. Then she began to play the 'Moonlight Sonata,' and at the end of the second movement she stopped again. 'Do you like that any better?' she asked.

Alec did not answer at once, and she rose from her seat, a little piqued at what she thought his rudeness. But Blake saw that he was trying to steady his voice before replying.

'Would you be so kind, if you don't mind the trouble,' he said in a very low tone, 'as to play that piece over again, from the beginning?'

Sophy consented, of course, and as she finished she asked Alec if he would care to hear anything else.

'Not just now, please ; anything else would sound coarse after that, wouldn't it?'

'Perhaps you are right,' said Sophy, with a smile.

'How happy you must be, to be able to play all that whenever you like!' exclaimed Alec.

'Do you think so? It is a very easy passage,' said Sophy, again a little at a loss how to answer her unconventional guest.

'Will you give us a song now?' asked Hubert.

But unfortunately Sophy chose one or two drawing-room songs of no musical character whatever; and as Alec thought them very poor, he was so much occupied in trying to find something to say that would not be absolutely rude, that he forgot to thank the performer; and Sophy noticed the omission.

'Well, what do you think of the young Scotchman, Sophy?' asked Hubert on his return to the drawing-room, after Alec had taken his leave.

Sophy raised her eyebrows, and dropped the corners of her mouth.

'I hardly know,' she replied. 'He is very unconventional; not commonplace certainly.

I rather like him. He has fine, expressive eyes. But he has no manners.'

'That will come in time,' said Hubert, stifling a yawn. 'You can't expect fine manners from a farmhouse.'

Hubert was right. As the months went on Alec unconsciously learned to adapt his manners to those of the Londoners. He lost, in part, the roughness of his Scottish speech ; and he insensibly acquired a more polished and conventional style of address. He visited not infrequently at Grove House, even when Blake was no longer to be found there ; and Sophy began to take quite a strong liking for him.

'Take care, Sophy,' said Hubert one day laughingly, as he noticed what good friend s the two had become; 'take care, or Alec's *beaux yeux* will be too much for you.'

Sophy turned away ; and Hubert thought she looked hurt, he didn't know why.

Alec had been at Messrs. Hatchett's office for some months, when one day, as he passed

through the outer office, Beattie came downstairs with a small sheaf of papers in his
hand.

'Where's MacGowan?' he asked sharply.

'He's not come down to-day yet, sir,'
answered one of the other clerks. 'I believe
he's not very well.'

Beattie made no reply, but his face wore
a very ugly look as he turned and left the
room.

' 'E'll get the sack *this* time, and no mistake,' Alec overheard one of the clerks say to
another, as he went out.

He went on to Lincoln's Inn, and on his
way back to the office he met MacGowan
coming, apparently, away from the office,
with a very miserable expression of countenance. He looked, indeed, a pitiable object,
even more dilapidated than usual, while his
pale face and trembling hands showed that
he had not yet recovered from the effects of
his last drinking-bout. Over his arm hung a

tattered coat, in which he had laboured at the desk for the last six years.

This garment he changed to his left arm on Alec's approach, and held out his right hand.

'Fareweel, Maister Lindsay,' said the poor fellow, with an air half sad, half comical. 'They've gien me the sack. That's the result o' bein' conveevial. Weel. It's a wide warl, an' a chancey; but we'll maybe foregather* again some day. Ye've been a guid freen' to me, Maister Lindsay. As for that sma' maitter o' the five shillin's ye lent me—perhaps ye'll allow me—tae——'

The sentence was artistically constructed. It was capable of being turned into an offer of repayment or a request that the matter might be allowed to stand over for a time, according as circumstances might direct; and it was accompanied by the production of an extremely shabby leathern purse, which evidently was but scantily furnished.

* Meet.

'Oh, never mind, never mind,' said Alec hastily. 'Any time will do for that—when you get rich. But has Mr. Hatchett really turned you away?'

'Aye; or raither that stuck-up deevil, Wullie Beattie. But I'll be even wi' him yet; him and his scunnersome* pride!'

'Have you any prospect of finding another situation?' asked Alec.

The other slowly but decisively shook his head.

'What will you do, then?'

For answer MacGowan carefully emptied his purse into his left palm, and took one or two coins out of the tiny heap.

'I owe this to my landlady,' he said, referring to the two sovereigns in his right hand.

There were only three or four left.

'And is that all you have between you and——'

MacGowan nodded.

* Disgusting.

25—2

'Stay here a minute,' said Alec, after a moment's thought. 'I'll see if I can make your peace for you. I can but try.' And without waiting for MacGowan's thanks he went on with quick steps to the office.

'So you have dismissed MacGowan,' said Alec as soon as he reached the managing clerk's room.

'Yes; lazy, drunken vagabond that he is!' said Beattie spitefully. 'I told him that I should not advise Mr. Hatchett to look over this offence; so I suppose he took that as equivalent to a dismissal.'

'But he will starve! He can't find another place without a character for steadiness; and he has only got three or four pounds in the world.'

'What's that to me?'

'Beattie, I wish you would give the poor fellow another chance,' said Alec, after a pause. 'You have only to say nothing of his absence, and it will never be noticed; or if you do mention it, say a word in excuse,

and I'm sure Mr. Hatchett would never think
of dismissing him.'

'Probably not,' said Beattie drily.

'Then why won't you do it?'

'Because I don't want a drunken imperti-
nent fellow like that about the place. And I
don't see why *you* need trouble yourself about
him;' and Beattie turned again to his papers
with something like a sneer on his face.

This was all that was needed to set Alec's
blood in a flame. He took a step or two
forward, his eyes in a blaze, his hands involuntarily clenched at his side.

'Then you prefer to be my enemy rather
than my friend?' he said, between his
teeth.

Beattie looked up in astonishment.

'What do you mean?' he asked.

'Only that I count no man my friend who
refuses me so small a favour.'

And Alec looked as if he meant to have
his way, whether it pleased Mr. William
Beattie or not.

Beattie was half inclined to laugh in the other's face, and · yet he was impressed in spite of himself. In one moment he had mentally run over the circumstances again. It was one of his maxims never to make an enemy if he could help it. Was it worth while making an enemy of young Lindsay? True, he saw no way in which Lindsay could injure him — things were rather the other way. But he might be a rich and influential man some day. He might have it in his power to refuse a request from *him*, or to advance his interests. These things passed through the managing clerk's mind in less than a second.

'Oh, if you put it in that way, Lindsay, to oblige you—I don't mind looking over it this time. But you'd better tell him this is his last chance. And I wish you would let me have the draft of Sir Joseph Wilson's settlement to-night if you can.'

Alec, who was secretly a little ashamed of his own vehemence, muttered a few words of thanks; and, going to his own room, scribbled on a piece of paper, 'Come back to your old seat, and say nothing about it.—A. L.' This he sent on to MacGowan by one of the clerks in the outer office.

'It doesn't matter,' said Beattie to himself, as Alec left him; 'the creature's sure to break out again in a month or two, so it comes very much to the same thing.'

As Alec left the office that night he found himself overtaken by MacGowan.

'Oh, Mr. Lindsay, sir!' cried MacGowan, 'I just canna thank ye ava'!'

'There's no need for that,' said Alec; 'but I may as well say this—I shan't be able to stand your friend another time; I shall not, indeed. And I very much fear that if you misbehave again, Mr. Beattie will turn you away for good and all.'

'I dare say, but I'll no gie him the chance. I'll swear to you I'll keep sober, Mr. Lindsay. I'll swear't to you on my Bible oath. I ken fine what gar'd him pack me awa'. The ither clerks ca'ed us " The Twa Scotties," him and me ; and he didna like it.'

' Well, I'm glad things have gone all right. Good-night,' said Alec, quickening his pace.

Before he had gone much farther he met Hubert Blake.

' By the way,' said Blake, when they had exchanged greetings, ' do you know whom I saw the other day in Regent Street—an old friend of yours—that young lady who used to stay with your uncle — what was her name ?'

' You mean Miss Mowbray,' said Alec quietly.

He spoke in his ordinary tone, but he could not prevent the quick blush mounting to his forehead.

After a few unimportant sentences Blake bade Alec good-night. A smile was on his lips as he turned away.

' Poor fellow !' he said to himself, ' so he has not forgotten her !'

CHAPTER XVIII.

AT THE ACADEMY.

ALEC had not, indeed, forgotten Laura Mowbray; though he had long since awakened from his first dream of love. Now, at twenty-two, he looked back on himself at nineteen as not only very young, but very foolish. He had half forgotten the episode of his wild declaration of love; but when he heard that Laura was near him once more, he was filled with a variety of emotions. At one time he determined to do nothing, to forget her if he could; at another time he was almost ready to set out and begin an insane search for her through the streets of London. He confessed to himself that though he had been intimate with Miss Mowbray he really knew her very slightly. He wanted to see her again, to learn something more of her; and yet he hesitated about deliberately setting to work to renew the old acquaintance.

As often happens in such a case, chance decided the matter for him. Two or three days after hearing that Laura was in town, Alec received a letter from his sister, in which she told him that their uncle James and his family had taken a furnished house in London, No. 21, Claremont Gardens, W., and meant to stay there some months.

The old man had become much more feeble during the last three years. And instead of making the best of things, and meeting the inevitable weakness of old age with a cheerful courage, he chose to consider himself a great invalid, and made his health the chief consideration of his life. This, of course, did not tend to improve either his health or his temper; and he had been for the last two years dragging his family about from one watering-place to another, to Aunt Jean's great disgust. She, good woman, was made of sterner stuff than her rich cousin. She did not approve of the unsettled life she was forced to lead; and she did not believe that her relative was even as much in need of care and attention as he really was.

As for Laura Mowbray, she possessed that enviable disposition (shared by people of all sorts and conditions) of making the best of things. She took care to keep out of her guardian's way when he was in a specially irritable mood; she flattered and soothed him not unsuccessfully now and then; she avoided Miss Lindsay as much as possible; and she seized upon every opportunity of amusing herself. She was by no means sorry to visit first one spa and then another, though she was forced to witness from the outside gaieties which no one asked her to share.

'One day,' she would say to herself, drawing her lips over her set teeth, as she sat listening to the band to which the other guests in the hotel were dancing. But she often received attentions from stray visitors, which helped in some degree to console her for the lack of amusements. When she heard that Mr. Lindsay had determined to spend some months in London, so as to secure the services of the famous Dr. Sheepshanks, Laura was overjoyed.

Of course Alec called to ask for his uncle, and he was quite shocked to find him looking so ill. His face was pinched and haggard, his hand thin and trembling; so that, to Alec's inexperienced eyes, it seemed as if death had already set his seal upon him. Old Mr. Lindsay was secretly pleased with Alec's demeanour. The young man could not express his concern, but it appeared plainly enough in his face and manner. He evidently believed that his great-uncle was in a condition demanding great care, sympathy, and consideration; and that was exactly what Mr. Lindsay wanted the world to believe concerning him. He made Alec sit down beside him, and asked him many questions in a feeble, piping voice, about his work, his prospects, and his ultimate aims. James Lindsay was entirely changed from the fussy, consequential, conceited being of three or four years before. Alec was almost touched by the meekness and painfulness (so to speak) of the old man's manner.

'That'll do now, Alec, my man,' he said, when he was at length tired of his companion. 'Go downstairs and see your aunt Jean.' (Here he sighed and lifted his eyebrows as if the very mention of that lady's name gave him an opportunity of exercising the virtue of patience.) 'Come and see me again soon. Good-day;' and he lay back as if exhausted, and closed his eyes.

Alec stole on tiptoe from the room, and went down to the drawing-room, where he found his aunt (as he called her) seated alone.

' I was very sorry to see Uncle James so poorly,' said Alec, as he took her hand.

Aunt Jean said nothing; but her sniff and look of contempt were sufficiently expressive.

'Don't you think my uncle very ill?' asked Alec, opening his eyes.

'He micht be waur,' said Aunt Jean.

She always spoke a broader dialect abroad than she did at home, as a protest against what she deemed the affectation and 'mim-mou'd' character of the English utterance.

'He seemed very weak,' said Alec, surprised and a little shocked at the old lady's want of sympathy.

'Maist fowk's no as strang at seventy-fower as they were at seventeen,' replied Aunt Jean, smoothing out her apron as she spoke.

Then the conversation turned upon other matters; and Alec began to fear that he would have to leave without seeing Laura. But just as he was preparing to go a knock was heard at the hall-door, and Laura came in from a stroll in the gardens.

She looked, it seemed to Alec, exactly the same as she had done when he last saw her. But he had not time to think of her looks. It was she herself, after these years—and three years are a long period to us all before we are four-and-twenty—standing before him. His heart beat as he took her hand, and though he was able to speak and look as if she were a mere ordinary acquaintance, each knew that it was not so. How far her old power over Alec was broken, Laura did not know; but she saw quite plainly, from a hundred little indications, that he was not indifferent to her. There was very little conversation, and such as there was was chiefly about trifles—the respective merits of Harrogate, Buxton, and Aix-le-Bains, the welfare of Alec's sister, and so on. Alec could not afterwards remember what they talked about, but he remembered the picture which Laura made, as she sat in a small, low chair at the window, playing with one of her gloves, and looking. Alec thought, more sweet and graceful than any human being had looked since his eyes had last rested upon her.

The next time Alec went to ask after his uncle, he found that his cousin, James Semple, had arrived from Glasgow, and was staying in the house. After a short visit to his uncle's sick-room, he was passing through the hall, when he met Semple and Miss Lindsay.

'You'll stay to lunch, Alec, and go with us to the Academy?' said Semple, when they had shaken hands. Miss Mowbray has had a friend come to see her—she is rather a swell at painting, and that sort of thing, I believe—and we intend going to the Academy as soon as we have finished lunch.

Alec thought it was very good-natured of Semple to propose that he should join the party, and he consented at once to stay. In a few minutes Laura and her friend, Miss Sewell, made their appearance; and only Alec's native sense of propriety prevented his staring at Miss Sewell with all his might.

She was very tall, very pale, and very thin, and she was dressed in a rather exaggerated form of the ' Greek ' costume. A broad scarf of the same material as her dress was carried across her breast, and fastened in some way upon her left shoulder. Her hair was gathered into a great knot at the back of her head ; and her sleeves were as tight as sleeves could by any possibility be. When she spoke it was in a languid, deliberate way, suggestive of refinement, and a superior delicacy of organization. Miss Lindsay regarded this young lady with mingled amazement and dislike ; and only a strong sense of her duty as hostess kept her from openly expressing her condemnation.

The conversation at table was not very brilliant.

' Are you fond of pictures, Miss Sewell ?' inquired Mr. Semple from the foot of the table.

Miss Sewell glanced slowly round at Laura, as if for enlightenment as to the purpose of so absurd a question, before she tranquilly replied :

'Everyone is, I suppose, Mr. Semple.'

But it was nearly impossible to make that gentleman feel that one was even trying to snub him.

'I don't know,' he replied; 'I know a lot of men, very intelligent men, who don't know a single one of the points of a picture. But art has made vast strides of late years : there's no denying that.'

Miss Sewell slowly and impressively turned her shoulder on Mr. Semple, and thenceforward ignored his existence.

It was not till the little party reached Burlington House that Alec understood the reason why he had been asked to join the party. Semple monopolized Laura, and Alec was expected to look after Miss Sewell.

The care of that young lady on such an occasion was no sinecure. She was full of enthusiasm, which was about one-tenth part real; and she found in nearly every picture some indication of genius.

' What an admirable tone there is in that little bit !' she would say.

Alec was dumb.

' Don't you think the breadth of effect there is perfectly wonderful ?' she asked, stopping before a great, aimless, carelessly-painted canvas.

' I'm afraid I—I don't know what you mean,' said Alec.

' The breadth, the feeling of vastness, of superiority to—to—you understand ?' replied Miss Sewell, in a very intense tone.

But Alec was staring at the picture.

' I don't know what a picture should be,' said he, very deliberately; ' but I know what a hillside *is*, and *that* thing has no resemblance to it whatever.'

' Oh, we must educate you, Mr. Lindsay,' said the girl, with a little laugh.

' I don't want to be educated !' said Alec stoutly. ' I think half the things here are coarse, stupid daubs, and half the rest are pretty, but senseless. They have no meaning. They don't help you to love beauty or nature more—not one bit.'

'Pray, sir,' said a caustic voice behind Alec, 'did you ever try to paint a picture ?'

An old man, with keen black eyes, deep-set under bushy gray eyebrows, was the speaker.

'Never in my life,' said Alec.

'Then you don't know how difficult it is to paint a good one.'

'I think it is wonderful that they are half as good as they are,' returned Alec.

The stranger stared, and the young man went on :

'I think it is wonderful that a man should be able to make likenesses of mountains, and seas, and clouds. But as men have learned how to do it, I think those who can't do it better than this,' pointing at a picture as he spoke, 'had better leave their work at home till they can make it more like nature. And at least they might choose beautiful or picturesque subjects, and not waste their time over tables and chairs, curtains and rugs, ladies' dresses and knick-knacks.'

The old man smiled grimly, and nodded once or twice as he turned away.

'Do find out who that is,' said Miss Sewell; 'I feel certain he is somebody.'

Miss Sewell was right. It was Sir Theodore Carson, the greatest painter of the day; and Miss Sewell at once resolved to profit by her experience and abandon enthusiasm for depreciation.

Meanwhile Semple had been asking his companion:

'Why does Miss Sewell dress in that absurd way?'

'You mustn't speak disrespectfully of my friend, sir,' said Laura. 'But dear Alice was always given to fancies. First she was learned and literary; then she was a regular athlete—she nearly ruined her health, trying to walk from London to Bath in two days— or five days, I forget which. Then she became original and classical, and slightly æsthetic. Next time I see her, she is sure to be something different.'

It was rather a tiresome afternoon for Alec; but it came to an end at last.

'What a handsome cousin you have, Laura!' said Alice Sewell to her friend in the privacy of her bedroom that afternoon.

'Do you think so? I never thought of Mr. Semple as particularly handsome.'

'I don't mean that fat, disagreeable-looking creature, you stupid girl! I mean the tall one, Mr. Alec Lindsay. He has beautiful eyes, and such a strong, independent way of speaking.'

'What a curious girl you are, Alice! I thought he would have been far too unconventional for you.'

'Don't you like him?' asked Alice in reply.

'Yes,' said Laura, in a hesitating way.

She was on the point of telling her friend that she had had Alec at her feet ; but she refrained.

'They are both in love with you,' said Alice tranquilly. 'Which do you mean to take ?'

'I'm afraid it must be the other one,' said Laura, turning away with a little sigh.

'Why ?'

'Oh, Alec has so little sense. He might have been his uncle's heir, I believe ; and he has simply neglected his interests. He will always be a poor man.' And the girl sighed again.

'And this Mr. Semple ?'

'Oh, he is pretty sure to be rich.'

'Don't decide too hastily, Laura, my dear,' said the elder girl. And Laura smiled, as much as to say that she perfectly understood the situation, and felt quite competent to direct her own affairs.

And in holding this opinion she only did herself justice.

CHAPTER XIX.

THE SHADOW OF DEATH.

As the weeks went by, Mr. James Lindsay grew slowly more feeble. He was no longer able to go out of doors, and he seldom left his room. He became more querulous and more capricious; and this disposition blinded his friends to his real danger.

But Dr. Sheepshanks saw the truth. He saw, also, that his patient had no idea that he was drawing very near the end of his life. And when a chance remark made the doctor aware that the old man had not yet made his will, he thought it was his duty to tell Miss Lindsay what the state of things really was.

'Danger!' she exclaimed, startled and

shocked by the doctor's words; ' it's not possible !'

' I am afraid there is no doubt of it, my dear madam.'

' But he's not an old man—not to say old. His father lived to ninety-three; and two of his uncles were past eighty.'

Dr. Sheepshanks only shook his head, with a grave professional smile.

' I never thought there was muckle wrang wi' him.'

' It is my decided opinion,' said the doctor, ' that Mr. Lindsay is not likely to live long. I think he ought to be told so, and advised to put his affairs in order.'

And thereupon Dr. Sheepshanks took his leave.

Miss Lindsay sat perfectly still for some minutes. She reproached herself for making light of her cousin's complaints; and felt that she was almost humiliated in being forced to bring to the invalid the unwelcome tidings. But it was clearly her duty. She rose suddenly, and went upstairs to his room.

'How are ye, Jeems?' she asked, sitting down by the bedside.

'Vera frail, Jean; I doubt I'm no long for this world. Did the haddies come frae Dundee?'

'Yes—but—the fact is, Jeems, I doubt ye're waur than I thocht ye.'

The sick man closed his eyes with a contented sigh. It was satisfactory to find that his obdurate relative at last believed that he was really ill. Miss Lindsay wanted to make some apology for her former attitude, but apologies did not come readily to her tongue.

'We ought a' to be prepared for our hinner en', Jeems,' she said at last.

Mr. Lindsay opened his eyes suddenly, and stared at his cousin. Such words from her meant something.

'What mak's ye say that?' he asked.

Aunt Jean moved uneasily in her seat and cleared her throat before replying.

' Weel, ye're no sae young as ye were, and life's an uncertain thing, and ye're vera far frae weel.'

The old man again closed his eyes, with a resigned expression of countenance. He had no idea of the truth. His cousin saw she must speak plainly.

' *And the doctor said I had better warn you.*'

The old man opened his eyes with a start, and stared at his companion. A look of horror crept into his face. He tried to speak, but the words would not come.

' Did the doctor say that?' he asked in a whisper.

' He did that,' said the old lady. ' I thocht it was no kindness to hide it from ye, Jeems.'

And after moving about restlessly for a few moments, she escaped from the room.

There was not a sound but the faint crackling of the coals in the grate, and the soft fall, now and then, of a cinder into the ashes.

He was to die. Few men can hear the

sentence unmoved, and James Lindsay was at heart a coward. He trembled at the thought of facing the unseen world—trembled as a murderer when the long-expected hand is suddenly placed on his shoulder.

For more than an hour he lay still, and his thoughts wandered back to the time when he was a ragged urchin at a little village school. He remembered the school-house well—the great tree under which he used to play. He remembered cheating a school-fellow once, and the thought of it troubled him. He wished he had confessed it and made restitution. It was impossible to make restitution now.

Then he saw himself a lad working for weekly wages. He recollected the happy accident which had given him the opportunity of making a fortune. He had been bold and energetic, and he had had his reward. Wealth, exceeding his wildest dreams, had been his. What good had it done to him? How few had been his pleasures! How empty his life ! And now he must leave it, and go forth into the darkness alone.

He tried to remember his good deeds, his church-going, his subscriptions to this or that fund, but they seemed to be all parts of the ordinary round of his existence, things he would have been ashamed not to do. Once, on a wet day, he had given a shilling to a beggar-woman, and she had blessed him for it. He was glad to think of that—but oh ! it was such a small thing !

He was startled by a knock at the door. It was Alec. The dying man looked at him with envy and something of bitterness. What would he not give for the lad's health and strength, for the years he had yet to live ?

'Alec,' said the old man suddenly, ' I want you to write a letter for me. Don't say anything about it : mind that. Write to Dr. Mackenzie, the Reverend Robert Mackenzie, D.D., the Free Gorbals Church, Glasgow, and tell him I want to see him instantly.'

The letter was soon written and despatched; and then James Lindsay felt somewhat easier.

It was Saturday afternoon when the letter reached Dr. Mackenzie's hands; and it sorely perplexed the worthy minister. If he were to put off his journey till Monday morning, he could not reach London before Monday night, and the delay might offend the rich man mortally. But starting at once would force him to intrust his flock to a very inferior preacher, and would, besides, involve the sin of travelling on the Sabbath. No doubt, if Mr. Lindsay were ill, the case would come within the saving clause of 'works of necessity or mercy.' He would then be justified in beginning a long journey on Saturday night. But how was he to be sure of Mr. Lindsay's state of health? He felt angry with the writer of the letter for not foreseeing the difficulty and giving more accurate information. Then he remembered that Mr. Lindsay had gone abroad for the sake of his health. What more likely than that he was very ill ? Dr. Mackenzie finally determined that it was an exceptional case, and that it would be clearly a work of mercy to hasten at once to the rich man's bedside.

He hunted up a minister who made a scanty living by filling the pulpits of his more fortunate brethren on emergencies like the present, and engaged him to preach twice at the Gorbals Free Church on the following day, and left Glasgow (not without some lingering doubts as to the legality of his proceedings) by the evening mail.

On Sunday forenoon he was standing by the bedside of his old acquaintance.

'It's very kind of ye to come, Doctor,' said Mr. Lindsay, in a feeble voice; 'but the Lord 'll reward ye.'

The minister thought that a mere earthly reward, at least to the extent of his travelling expenses, would likewise be desirable; but he merely answered:

'I'm sorry to find you going down the hill, Mr. Lindsay.'

'Ay, it's a road we maun a' travel, Doctor. They tell me I'm near the end o't.'

'And I trust you are at peace in your mind ?'

'Not as I would like—not as I would like to be, Dr. Mackenzie.'

'Ye should rest on the promises, my friend,' said the minister, and he repeated various texts of the Bible bearing upon the forgiveness of sins.

The old man listened almost impatiently.

'I ken a' that,' he said, as the minister ended.   'I havena been an elder of the Free Kirk thirty years for nothing.   But how am I to ken they apply to me ?'

'They are for all men,' answered the minister.

'Just so ; but all men are not saved.'

'Because they do not believe.'

'If I believe I'm saved, I *am* saved ? That's about it, it seems to me.'

'I wouldn't put it in that way.   There is such a thing as false assurance.'

' Then how am I to know that mine is not a false assurance ?' and the old man looked anxiously in the minister's face.

' You have only to accept forgiveness as a free gift, and it is yours,' said the other, falling back on his formula.

' But surely I must repent of my sins ?'

' Of course.'

' But I don't know that I do repent—that is, not as I should. And after all, Doctor, it's not what I have done that troubles me, so much as what I have not done. You don't remember any texts, now, bearing on that ?'

Dr. Mackenzie frowned, and took a pinch of snuff.

' I can't just say that I do—not at this moment,' he said at last. ' But I don't think you have any cause to reproach yourself on that score, Mr. Lindsay ; you have always subscribed liberally to the Sustentation Fund, the Aged Ministers' Scheme, and the Missionary Society. I don't think you have any special cause for alarm.'

But the sick man looked dissatisfied.

'I've been thinking, Doctor, what I should do wi' my siller,' he said. Dr. Mackenzie was all attention. 'I've none nearer me than Lindsay o' the Castle Farm ; and he's a man of nearly my own age. He doesna want a great heap o' siller. If I leave him enough to free his land, and maybe buy back one o' the auld farms, it will be plenty. Then there's my nephews. What would be the use o' making these young men rich all on a sudden ? They would only waste the money. Better to let them work for it.'

'I quite agree with you,' said Dr. Mackenzie heartily.

'I'm not so rich as folk say,' went on Mr. Lindsay ; 'but after providing for my relations in a small way, I have a good deal left. Doctor, do you think it would mak' up for things a bit, if I was to leave five hundred thousand to the Free Kirk ?'

The minister was more than astonished. He started and drew a long breath.

'What do you think?' asked the old man anxiously.

'I cannot just say it would mak' up for things. We have no merits of our own, ye ken. They are all but filthy rags. But it's a grand idea, and well worth tryin' !'

This was not the solid encouragement for which Mr. Lindsay had hoped.

'It will doubtless redound to your credit, and win ye an increase of glory,' said the minister again, noticing his penitent's disappointed look.

The sick man sighed. He would have been satisfied at that moment if he could have felt certain of a very moderate share of glory.

'You think so?' he asked anxiously.

'I am certain of it.'

'Then I'll do it !' exclaimed the old man, striking his fist on the bedclothes. 'I'll send for a lawyer the first thing in the morning. How do you think it should be left ?'

'I would vest it in trustees, for the general

27—2

purposes of the Church, to be used at their discretion.'

'Very well. Will you be one of the trustees?'

Dr. Mackenzie was prepared for this question, and he had already decided to decline the honour. He did not see how even the smallest pecuniary benefit would flow to him from accepting it.

'I think I would rather not,' he replied. 'One should always appoint young men as trustees. But, if you have no objection, I would consent to be secretary to the trust. If you were to mention my name in the will, now, just recommending me to the trustees as their secretary, I would really be much obliged.'

'I'll do that,' said Mr. Lindsay. He quite understood the minister's reasons for choosing the humbler post, and thought none the less of his friend for this display of prudence. 'Of course you'll stop here as long as you can; it will be a comfort to me. I'll tell Miss Lindsay to get your room ready.'

Dr. Mackenzie said that he would, and reflected, as he went downstairs, that it would be a comfort to himself to stay till the will was duly executed.

In the library he found Alec, who often found his way to Claremont Gardens on a Sunday morning, partly because it was an excuse to himself for not going to church alone, partly because there was always a chance that he might be able to accompany Miss Lindsay and Laura to some place of worship. On this occasion he had been disappointed. No one had stirred out since the morning; and he was idly turning over the pages of the *Saturday Review* when the minister entered the room.

'I believe you are Dr. Mackenzie,' said Alec, getting up and holding out his hand.

'Yes. I don't remember to have had——'

'Oh, it was I who wrote and asked you to come.'

'Ah! just so. You have not gone to church to-day, Mr. Alexander.'

'No,' returned Alec shortly, returning to his seat.

'Whom do you generally sit under in London?   Dr. Bruce? or Mr. Martin?'

'Neither.   I sometimes go to St. Paul's, oftener to Westminster Abbey.'

Dr. Mackenzie frowned heavily.

'Is the Gospel preached there, Mr. Alexander?' he said in a tone that was meant to be one of deep solemnity.

'I really can't say.   I suppose so.'

'You go chiefly for the music, perhaps.'

'Partly, no doubt.'

'For the gratification of a sensuous taste! the indulgence of a carnal delight!   There is no spiritual worship in such places—none! It is turning the house of God into a concert-room; nothing less!   Ah! this country was never properly reformed.   It was done in a very half-hearted way.   We want a new Reformation, that shall sweep away the remnants of idolatrous practices that yet defile what is nominally Protestant worship.'

The minister walked up and down the little room in his excitement, gesticulating as he went, to the manifest peril of a statuette on a bracket.

Alec rose, and gravely removed the ornament to a place of safety.

'No great harm if the heathen image had been knocked down,' said Dr. Mackenzie grimly. 'And let me tell you, young gentleman, that the best of Scotland's sons have been those who were loyal to her reformed and Scriptural form of church government and public worship.'

'Perhaps so,' said Alec, seeing that he was expected to say something. 'I know a good many, however, who have not done so.'

'You know a good many young Scotchmen in London, perhaps?'

'A good many.'

'And are not those who are faithful to their early training Sabbath-keepers, church-goers —I don't mean church-concert-goers—are

they not respected and prosperous, and successful in their business ?'

'They are,' said Alec, 'and not one of them
now believes what he was brought up to
believe.'

'What ? What do you say ? How can
you decide on a point that must lie between
each man and his Maker ?'

'Because I have asked them,' answered
Alec. 'Each chooses his own road. Some
differ from the orthodox Presbyterian belief
on one point, some on another, but none hold
it in its entirety.'

'There are many non-essential points,'
began the minister ; but he was not sorry
that at this point the door opened, and Miss
Lindsay, followed by Laura, entered the room.

Presently luncheon was announced, and
Semple, who was just then paying one of
his frequent visits from Glasgow, joined the
others on their way to the dining-room.

The minister's 'blessing' was of a kind
more usual in Scotland forty years ago than

it is now. He prayed for the master of the house, and for all his necessities, and for various spiritual and temporal blessings for each member of the household. Suddenly he seemed to remember the object with which he had started, and came to an abrupt conclusion with an adaptation of the usual formula.

Various subjects of conversation were begun in a languid way, but Dr. Mackenzie ingeniously and successfully turned them all into a religious channel in a very short space of time. He did not approve, upon principle, of any conversation on Sunday upon matters of a more profane nature than the merits of popular preachers, the existence or non-existence of Sunday-schools and Bible-classes in various places, the spread of Presbyterianism in England, and similar topics. As soon as anyone wandered away to secular subjects, Dr. Mackenzie went out, and headed him, so to speak, and drove him back.

The meal proved, in consequence, a dull one, and matters did not improve when it was

over and the little party returned to the
library.

'Folk don't keep the Sabbath as they used
to do in my young days,' said Miss Lindsay, with a weak attempt to propitiate the
minister.

'So much the worse for them, ma'am,' said
Dr. Mackenzie.

'When I was a young woman, everybody
attended both diets of worship. Walking for
pleasure on the Sabbath, reading story-books,
and the like, was never heard of.'

'Of course not; but the old godly ways
are deserted now. Do you think it is a right
thing to read such a paper as that on this holy
day?' he continued, speaking to Alec, who
had thoughtlessly picked up the *Saturday
Review*.

'I see no harm in it,' returned Alec
shortly.

He looked up and saw Semple, who (fortunately for him) was out of Dr. Mackenzie's
range of vision, lay down one of Ouida's

novels, making a grimace at Laura as he did so.

' You defy the law of God, then, and choose the portion of the Sabbath-breaker. You——'

' Dr. Mackenzie,' said Alec quietly, ' have I presumed to pass judgment on your actions, and condemn them ?'

The minister only stared.

' You do not pretend to any sacerdotal authority, I believe ?'

' Certainly not.'

' Then by what power or authority, I may ask, do you claim to interfere with me ?'

And having said this, Alec tossed the newspaper aside and left the room, with the words ' law of God,' ' Fourth Commandment,' 'judgment,' ringing in his ears.

After ascertaining that his uncle had fallen asleep, Alec went off to his own lodgings in no very Christian frame of mind. And Dr. Mackenzie neither forgot nor forgave the way in which the reprobate (as he considered him) had received his timely reproof.

CHAPTER XX.

MR. LINDSAY'S WILL.

EARLY the following morning Dr. Mackenzie despatched a note in Mr. Lindsay's name to Messrs. Hatchett, Small, and Hatchett, asking that one of the firm should call upon him as soon as possible, and take his instructions for the making of his will. This note was delivered in the afternoon, and was in due course passed on to Mr. Beattie, with the words pencilled across it, 'Please attend to this at once.' Mr. Hatchett and Mr. Small were both too important men to attend in person and take instructions for a will, and the junior partner happened to be in America.

'Ah!' said Beattie to himself, as he glanced

at the note, 'this will decide our friend Lindsay's future. I wonder whether Semple will
come in for a good share. Surely, if he does,
he won't trouble me about that six hundred I
owe him ?'

About four o'clock Beattie presented himself
at Mr. Lindsay's house, and was at once
shown up to the sick man's chamber.

'Are you Mr. Hatchett, or Mr. Small ?'
was Mr. Lindsay's first question.

'Neither. My name is Beattie. I am the
managing clerk of the conveyancing department. It was quite impossible for one of the
partners to come to-day ; and as you seemed
to wish your will made at once——'

'Oh, very well, sit down,' interrupted the
old man.

He was by no means pleased that a clerk
had been sent to him ; but it was not worth
while to dispute the point.

Beattie found writing materials on a side-
table, and seated himself at the bedside, with
his pen in his hand.

'First of all, sir,' he began, 'I shall want your full name and address.   By the way, you have lived here for some months, I believe ?'

'Yes.'

'And you have no intention of returning to Scotland ?'

'No,' said the old man grimly.

'I mean, if you recover ?'

'Not permanently.'

'Have you any will now existing ?'

'No.'

For some minutes there was silence, and then Mr. Lindsay named the two friends whom he wished to be his trustees and executors. Then there was a longer pause.   At last the sick man broke the silence, speaking rapidly, as if he feared that even then he might change his mind.

'Sell my houses, and all that's in them— nobody will care for them after I am gone. Sell the oil-works at Drumleck, and the business.   They have been mismanaged sadly of late ; besides, the trade is not what it was, and I doubt if there's much more to be made in it,' he added, as if speaking to himself. ' Then my brother, Alexander Lindsay, of the Castle Farm, Muirburn, must have ten thousand pounds. And my second cousin, Jean Lindsay, who has been my housekeeper for many years, ten thousand. Have you put that down ?'

' Yes.'

' To my niece, Margaret Lindsay, three thousand, and to my ward, Laura Mowbray, say two thousand. I pity that lassie's husband,' he added, under his breath.

Again there was a long pause, so long that Beattie dried his writing, and looked up as if to ask whether the instructions were ended.

' And I bequeath,' said the old man in a firm voice, ' to all those who have been Moderators of the General Assembly of the Free Church of Scotland, to the present Moderator, and to every succeeding Moderator, the sum of five hundred thousand pounds, in trust for the Free Church of Scotland, to be

used, at their discretion, for the general purposes of that body.'

Mr. Lindsay glanced at the lawyer as he
pronounced these words, that he might see
what effect the magnitude of the bequest had
upon him ; but, to the old man's disappointment, Mr. Beattie's face remained perfectly
impassive. 'For the general purposes of
that body,' he repeated, writing down the
words.

'And I request these trustees to appoint
my friend the Rev. Robert Mackenzie, D.D.,
Secretary to the Trust, at such reasonable
salary as they may think fit. And, by the
way, I leave the said Rev. Robert Mackenzie
one thousand pounds, for himself. The rest
of my property—what do you call it ?'

'The residue.'

'Ay. The residue I leave to my nephews,
James Semple and Alexander Lindsay, equally
between them. I calculate that will give them
some ten thousand apiece.'

'By the way, have you personal property

to the extent of half a million ?' inquired the clerk.

' Yes.'

' I only asked, because otherwise there might be a difficulty about the Statutes of Mortmain. But I can make the legacy to the Free Church come out of the personalty. Have you any further instructions ?'

' No.'

' Then I will read over what I have written, and if it is in accordance with your wishes, you will please initial it.'

This was done, and Beattie took his leave, promising that the draft would be ready in a day or two.

As he reached the hall, he met James Semple, who was coming out of the library.

' Come in here a moment, Beattie,' said Semple, drawing him into the room, which was empty. ' What have you been about with my uncle ?'

' I can't speak of a client's business, you know,' answered Beattie with a smile.

' Oh, stuff! Don't come the virtuous to such an extent as that. Weren't you taking down his instructions for his will ?'

Beattie smiled again.

' Really, my dear fellow, consider my position,' he began.

' I am certain you were. Now, look here. Am I to have the business at Drumleck, or am I not ?'

But the other was dumb.

' We can't talk here,' said Semple nervously. ' It's past five ; there's no necessity for you to go back to the office, is there ?'

' No.'

' Then, will you come and dine with me at the Cosmopolitan, say at half-past six ? I can't very well ask you to dine here, you know.'

Beattie accepted the invitation. He knew very well that Semple's object in giving it was to extract information from him about the will ; and Semple told himself that if Beattie had not meant to yield, he would not

have promised to dine with him. But
Beattie had by no means made up his mind
on the point. One thing, however, he hardly
needed to decide—he did not intend to sell
his information for nothing.

Semple secured a private room at the
Cosmopolitan, and ordered a good dinner and
the best wine procurable.

There was but little conversation between
the two young men during dinner; but as
soon as the meal was concluded, Semple's
impatience made him open the subject which
was uppermost in their minds.

'Look here, Beattie,' he began; 'I've
been a good friend to you, haven't I?'

'Yes, you have, Semple.'

'I lent you six hundred pounds, you
know — about that matter — on very bad
security.'

'You did.'

'Well, fill your glass, old man.'

Beattie obeyed; but the other noticed that
he merely put the glass to his lips.

28—2

'Come now, Beattie,' said Semple, 'I really think you might oblige me in that little matter we were speaking of. You see, I want to have a talk with my uncle about it; but I must first know what his ideas are.'

'How could I do such a thing? Suppose Hatchett's people were to get wind of it, what would be the consequence?'

'Tuts, man! they can never know of it!'

'I should be ruined.'

'There's not the slightest chance of it.'

'I should be constantly in your power.'

'That means you want to drive a bargain with me.'

'I thought you might sign this, perhaps,' said Beattie, drawing a paper from his pocket.

It was a receipt in full for six hundred pounds.

'Well, you *are* cool!' cried Semple, greatly admiring his friend's impudence.

' Will you sign it ?'

' Of course not. I should be mad to do such a thing. Why, I can ask my uncle at any time what his intentions are.'

' Then why come to me ?' asked Beattie slowly, lifting his eyebrows.

' It would be convenient to know before-hand, certainly ; but it's not worth that,' said Semple.

' I think you'll find it's worth a good deal,' said the other, smiling again.

This whetted Semple's curiosity, and roused his anxiety.

' Come now, let me see the instructions—I know you have the paper about you—and I'll let you off a hundred.'

' And not trouble me for the balance for three years ?'

' Well, yes ; and that's all I'll do. I've made up my mind.'

Beattie saw that no better terms were to be obtained, so he rang for pen and ink, altered the word ' six ' into ' one ' in the receipt with which he had provided himself, and then it was signed.

'Now,' said Semple.

Without speaking a word, Beattie drew the paper of instructions from his pocket, and laid it on the table.

Semple snatched it up hastily ; and the other sat watching him, knocking off, now and then, the ash from the end of his cigarette with his little finger.

Semple ran hurriedly through the first part of the document ; then suddenly he gave a cry, and started up, as white as a sheet.

'Sit down, man,' said Beattie, almost alarmed at the expression on his companion's face. 'Sit down, and drink this,' and he poured him out a glass of port.

Semple took it with a hand that trembled so as to spill the wine, and drank it off. Then he burst out in a torrent of imprecations.

'I knew that —— old minister would make him put down something for his religion, but I never dreamt of such madness as this !'

Beattie said nothing ; on the whole he rather enjoyed his friend's discomfiture.

'It's infamous ! And I, to have slaved all my life for nothing—nothing, by —— ! That half-million is about all he has.'

'You are to have half the residue, you see,' said Beattie ; 'about ten thousand pounds, I believe.'

'And what's that ? He might as well have left me ten thousand farthings ! I ought to have had a hundred thousand pounds at least. But I won't submit to it ! I will not. I will dispute the will. My uncle is not in a fit state of mind to make a will. Eh, Beattie ?'

Beattie was leaning with his arms on the table, as he slowly pressed the end of his cigarette against the ash-tray. On hearing his companion's last words, he slowly shook his head without looking up.

'When I saw him this afternoon, Mr·

Lindsay was in perfect possession of his faculties,' he said calmly. (The other darted at him a look of contempt.) 'And the doctor who attends him, as well as his relations and servants, would no doubt be of the same opinion,' he added firmly.

Semple dropped his eyes on the table, and was silent.

'Is there no one who has influence with him, no one who might induce him to alter his mind ?' added the young lawyer, after a pause.

'Nobody in the world,' said Semple bitterly. 'My uncle is the very incarnation of self-conceit and obstinacy. Everybody will talk of this "munificent bequest," and that's all he cares for. I will try, of course, what I can do ; but there's not the slightest chance——'

'Take care that you don't let him see that you know his intentions before he speaks of them himself,' said Beattie anxiously.

'You needn't be afraid,' said the other.

There was silence in the room for some
minutes, while Semple sat brooding over the
prospect before him, his eyes on the floor.
Suddenly he started to his feet, and, striking the table with his fist, cried, with an
oath :

'I won't stand it ! I will not ! I'm not
going to be fooled out of all this money after
toiling for it so long. Beattie, you must
help me to get it. There are ways and
means. You lawyers know them. I'll take
any reasonable risk myself, and you shall
have half - profits — that is, two hundred
thousand out of the five. That's fair, isn't
it ?'

Beattie smiled contemptuously.

'May I ask you what you were thinking
of ?' he inquired, with mock politeness.

'I'm thinking of getting the money,' said
Semple roughly. 'And if you're too much
of a coward to help me, I'll find someone
who will ! Think, man. Is there no way ?
Can't we find someone who'—here he

dropped his voice to a whisper—'who could imitate the signature, you know.'

'And find ourselves in a convict prison for the rest of our lives ? No, thank you.'

'But it's awful to think of such a sum slipping away from one like that. It's a sin not to make an effort——'

Here Mr. Semple stopped ; his ideas were getting rather mixed.

'You'll think it over,' said he, after a long pause.

'I'll think it over,' repeated the other.

'Then you think there's a chance of——'

'A chance ? Well, hardly that. And yet, as you say, it would be a pity to miss an opportunity of—two hundred thousand pounds, I think you said ?'

'If I take the risk, one hundred thousand, Beattie. It's a large sum.'

'Well, I'll think it over. Good-night,' said Beattie, abruptly holding out his hand. 'By the way,' he added, turning back as he reached the door, ' you had better give me a

call to-morrow morning, before I go down to
the office, for there's no time to lose. I will
expect you at half-past eight. Something
may have occurred to me in the meantime.'

It happened that that very evening Alec
Lindsay called at his uncle's, and as soon as
the old man was aware that his nephew was
in the house, he sent for him.

'Alec,' he said, 'sit down. I have something to say to you.'

Alec obeyed, wondering what was coming.

"I am decidedly of opinion,' said Mr.
Lindsay, in his old pragmatical way, 'that it
is not a good thing for a young man to be
made suddenly rich. If he has enough to
give him a start in life, that is all he needs.
Wealth is often the occasion of a young man's
ruin. Therefore I have not made you my
heir.'

'I hope you never thought I was expecting
anything of the kind,' said Alec quickly.

'No. So you won't be disappointed. I
have not forgotten you in my will. You will

have a competency. I have not forgotten any of my relations who had natural claims on me. But I have thought it right to leave the bulk of my property to the Kirk. The will is not drawn up yet. I had a man here to-day from your office, taking down the heads of what I want done. I must say I think one of the partners might have come.'

'They are very much engaged.'

'So this Mr. Beattie said. But I don't want to have a clerk that I don't know anything about attending to such an important matter. I should like you to see to it yourself. You do that sort of work in the office, don't you?'

'Yes—but—— The fact is, uncle, I had rather not meddle with it, especially if my name is to be in the will.'

'Tuts, man, what does that signify?'

'Not much in reality, but——'

'You can tell one of the partners that it is my wish.'

'That would be a very awkward thing for me to do.'

'You're very particular. It's not such a great favour to ask of you. Will you do it if I write to the firm, and say I prefer that you should draw up the will?'

'Yes, uncle. I am very willing to oblige you ; but if you are really anxious that I should do it, you had better write to the firm about it.'

'Then I will write a note now, and have it posted to-night, so that they may get it in the morning. That's all I wanted to say to you. Just ask your aunt Jean to come here for a minute, when you go down.'

Alec found Miss Lindsay sitting with Laura in the library, and delivered his message.

'What secrets have you and my uncle been discussing?' asked the girl, as soon as the elder lady had left the room.

(Laura had dropped into the way of calling

Mr. Lindsay 'uncle,' though no relationship existed between them.)

'None that I know of,' answered Alec.

'Come now, don't tell me a fib,' said Laura, smiling, and holding up her forefinger. ' You shouldn't try to be deceitful. It is of no use, for your face betrays you. There was a stranger here this afternoon, a dark, silent kind of man. He came to see uncle, and I believe it was to make his will. Am I not right ?'

' Possibly.'

' Of course I am. My guesses are always right. I wonder who is to be the favoured one ? I do hope it will be you, Alec !'

' Thank you,' he answered with some confusion.

'Ah ! I see you know all about it. Uncle and you were talking it over just now, weren't you ?'

' If we were, you know I can't speak of what passed between us.'

' Oh, I know that, of course. Still, I am

a little curious. Not with regard to myself, personally. I have no right to expect that Mr. Lindsay should leave me anything, for after all (though he has been as kind as any blood-relation could be to me), he and I are not related. You remember my·telling you that, the first time we met ? You remember that night ? You sat next me at dinner, and your cousin was so jealous of my talking to you !'

'Yes, I remember that night very well.'

'But I *should* like to know that uncle had done his duty by you. He has so much money ; and as you are his favourite nephew, he is certain to leave you quite a large sum.'

'I don't see that at all. I mean, I have no claim on him whatever.'

'Oh yes! you have,' said Laura ; but she stopped suddenly, for Miss Lindsay just then returned to the room.

As Alec went home that night, Laura's image remained with him. And more than once the thought occurred to him, that if his uncle carried out his intention of leaving him a substantial sum, it would bring the possibility of his winning Laura Mowbray a little nearer.

CHAPTER XXI.

ROGUES IN COUNCIL.

As James Semple went to keep his early appointment with the lawyer's clerk on the following morning, his great fear was that Beattie might in the meantime have changed his mind. For himself, his indignation and rage knew no bounds. He felt ready to run any risks. But he knew that without the aid of his astute friend he was powerless; and the sense of his impotence only added to his anger.

'Well, here you are,' said Beattie, when Semple was shown into his room. 'Sit down, and have a cup of coffee.'

'I don't mind if I do. And you might

put a dash of brandy in it. It's terribly cold to-day. Don't you find it so?'

'No.'

'I dare say not. You'd find no weather cold; you're cold-blooded, like a leech.'

As soon as the two men were left alone together, Semple drew his chair nearer to Beattie's and leant forward.

'Have you thought of anything?' he asked in a whisper.

Beattie looked at the other's hungry, wolfish eyes, and turned away, half in disgust.

'It seems to me, as you said last night, almost a sin not to try to prevent so gross an act of folly as the one we were speaking of,' he said at last. 'And a plan has occurred to me that might possibly succeed.'

'Really! You're a brick, Beattie. I always said you were. I always knew you had twice as much brains as most fellows.'

Beattie took no notice of this.

'There is a risk about it, no doubt. There

always must be in such cases. But I think the danger may be reduced to a minimum.'

'What is it? What is your idea?'

'It will require some care and adroitness on your part, when the critical moment arrives; but I shall ask you to do nothing impossible, or even difficult.'

'I can't do any forg——, if you mean that,' said Semple, with a slight shiver. 'I really couldn't. I mean, I haven't the skill.'

Beattie threw a contemptuous glance at his companion.

'You surely forget what I said on that point last night,' he said coldly.

'But how else are you to manage it? What is your idea?'

'I may as well tell you now that I don't take another step unless you give me back that promissory note of mine. You can sign a receipt for the money now, and send me the note when you return to Glasgow. I will burn them both. "Dead men tell no tales."'

'Oh, but you know, old man, that's too much. I let you off a hundred only last night.'

'What has that to do with it? I gave you a return for the hundred, didn't I? I tell you I have made up my mind that the old debt must be cleared out of the way to begin with, and I must have half profits if we succeed.'

'Half profits! Why, you couldn't touch a penny of it without me!'

'Nor could you without me.'

And after a little wrangling, Semple was forced to consent to these conditions.

'Now, what is your precious plan?' he asked, when he had signed the necessary paper.

'I think you had better leave that to me,' said Beattie, as he lit a cigarette.

'That's cool, I must say!'

'As you like,' answered the other, shrugging his shoulders; 'but it seems to me that it's much safer for you to know nothing. I may very probably want your help. But in case of anything coming out, the less you know the better.'

'I see. All right.'

'There is one unfortunate circumstance. We can't secure the whole half-million. We can only get about half of it.'

'Half of it! Why didn't you tell me that sooner? Do you think I would have gone shares with you, if I had known that? I won't do it, and that's flat.'

Semple could be obstinate enough when he liked; and in the end a compromise was effected. If Semple realized two hundred thousand pounds from his uncle's estate, Beattie was to have half of the whole. All above two hundred thousand the former was to keep for himself.

'And now you had better go, as I must go down to the office,' said Beattie. 'Well, it's worth the risk,' he muttered to himself when he was left alone. 'A hundred thousand pounds. A very fair sum. Enough to be

the foundation of a first-rate fortune.' And
with this pleasant thought in his mind he
set out for Theobald's Road.

Mr. Hatchett was before him that morning,
and was busy opening letters when he
arrived.

'There's a note from that Mr. Lindsay
whom you saw last night,' said the solicitor,
tossing it across the table. 'He wants his
nephew to draw his will. He can do it, I
suppose?'

Beattie stood with the note in his hand
without answering.

'It doesn't matter how it is done, for of
course you will send the draft to counsel.'

'There won't be time for that, I'm afraid,'
said Beattie slowly.

'Ah! The old man is dying, is he?
Then you can look over the draft yourself,
you know.' And Mr. Hatchett began speaking about another matter, to which the
managing clerk was forced to give his
attention.

When the interview was over, Beattie went
to his own room, and throwing on the table
the letters and papers which he carried, he
sat down and leant his head upon his hand.
Then he took up a pen and began idly drawing lines from one blot to another on his
writing-pad. Did Alec Lindsay know of this
whim of his uncle's ? Probably he did.
And if he did not, would it be safe to disre-
gard it ? These were the questions that were
troubling him.

He was still sitting in the same attitude
when a knock came to the door. He started
up, and drew one of the papers towards him,
as if he were reading it.

'Come in !' he cried, and Alec Lindsay
walked into the room.

'Good morning, Beattie. Have you seen
the letters to-day ?'

'Yes.'

'Was there one from my uncle ?'

'Yes; I saw it.'

'It's a great nuisance,' said Alec, seating

himself on a corner of the table. 'I had very much rather not have anything to do with drawing the will, especially as I believe I am to be one of the legatees.'

'It is hardly usual, certainly. But you are rather busy just now, I think. I'll do the will for you if you like.'

'Thank you. But my uncle made me promise that I would see to it myself. I will send the draft to counsel.'

'There isn't time for that,' said Beattie in a decided tone. 'Mr. Battiwell would keep the draft for a week—three days at least—and your uncle particularly wished it done at once. If anything should happen in the meantime——'

'I see. Well, you will look over the draft after I have done it?'

'If you like. But it's the easiest thing in the world. A child might do it. You have nothing to do but follow the precedent. By the way,' he added, 'I suppose your uncle has told you of his intentions?'

'He told me he meant to leave the bulk of his property to the Free Church.'

'What can have put such an absurd notion into his head?'

'Well, I fancy a Dr. Mackenzie, who is staying with him just now, may have had something to do with it.'

'Ah! A minister, I suppose. Your uncle is a good deal under his influence, I dare say?'

'No; I don't think so. And really I don't know that Dr. Mackenzie even suggested it.'

'Well, it's no business of mine,' said Beattie, shrugging his shoulders.

'Will you give me the paper of instructions?' said Alec, after a pause.

'Certainly; here it is.' And Mr. Beattie turned to the other documents before him, with an air that said, 'I have wasted too many minutes already.'

But as soon as Alec had left the room, he relapsed into his former attitude. Presently he rose and paced up and down the room with slow, cat-like steps. Then he paused at the window, and stood there for more than half an hour, looking out at the blank wall opposite him. 'That might do,' he said to himself at last, as he turned away. 'It ought to succeed. There is a risk, certainly; but we can't help that.'

Then Mr. Beattie put on his hat, and going to a telegraph-office some little way off, he sent this message to his friend James Semple:

'Meet me at the Cosmopolitan this afternoon at four o'clock.'

About three o'clock he went into Alec Lindsay's room.

'Well, how are you getting on with the will?'

'The draft is nearly finished. I have not been able to go on with it steadily, or it would have been done sooner. Will you look over it now?'

'You can put it on my table when it is

ready. I suppose you will send it to your
uncle to-night ?'

'Yes. I will send it by to-night's post.'

'You had better say in your note that if
the draft is satisfactory it may be returned to
us to-night, and we will bring it to be
executed on Thursday morning. There will
be plenty of time to have it engrossed to-
morrow.'

'Very well. I will do that.'

'And, I say, Lindsay, I think you had
better not send it to the law stationer's.'

'Why ?'

'Because the man who copied your draft at
the law stationer's would be sure to speak of
it. How foolish your uncle would look if a
paragraph about his bequest got into the
papers, and if he afterwards changed his mind,
as very likely he may do.'

Alec shook his head.

'You don't know my uncle, or you wouldn't
talk of his changing his mind. But I'll give
it to one of the fellows in the office to engross.'

'It is much better to have things of that sort copied in the office.'

With these words Beattie left the room, and shortly afterwards he quietly went out.

When Alec finished the draft, he took it to the managing clerk's room, and as no one was there he left it on the table as he had been told to do. About five o'clock he wrote the note to his uncle which Beattie had suggested to him, and he told the clerk whose duty it was to post the letters that Mr. Beattie would give him the document that was to be sent with the note. Having done this, Alec went home.

The clerk found the draft of the will on Mr. Beattie's table. He was not quite sure that his superior had seen it, for Mr. Beattie was not in the office ; but thinking he might be held responsible if the letter were delayed, he sent it off with the draft.

'Do you know that your uncle had specially desired that Alec Lindsay should draw his will ?' were Beattie's first words to his friend, when he met him at the restaurant at four o'clock.

'No! Then the game is up!'

'I'm not so sure of that. There is a chance yet. It will depend on your skill and coolness.'

'On mine! I thought you said I was to know nothing, and do nothing.'

'And wait till the gold fell into your lap, eh?' sneered Beattie. 'I shall have my own share of trouble, and danger too, I can tell you. You may believe me that if I could do it all myself, I wouldn't risk leaving it to you.'

'Then why don't you do it?'

'Do I live at No. 21, Claremont Gardens?' asked Beattie savagely.

'What do you want me to do?' asked the other.

'I'll tell you when the time comes. But why did you leave me to find out about this minister, this Dr. Mackenzie? Why didn't you tell me about him?'

'I didn't think it was of any importance.'

'Of no importance! I suppose he knows all about your uncle's intentions?'

'I suppose he does.'

'Anybody else?'

'Not that I know of. I think not.'

'Very well. Now listen to me. The draft of the will will be sent to your uncle to-night, with a request that it should be returned by to-night's post. It will be delivered about eight or nine o'clock, I imagine. Your business will be to keep this Dr. Mackenzie out of the way. Take him to some meeting— anywhere, in fact, but keep him out of the house till your uncle has sent back the draft to us. You understand?'

'Yes; I'll see what I can do.'

'You'll do nothing of the kind. You'll *do it.*'

'I don't know why you should speak in that way to me, Beattie!'

'Neither do I. All I know is, that no one must see the draft except your uncle himself.'

'I suppose I may read it, if he offers it to me?'

'No. Make some excuse, and don't look at it. I know all that is in it. And remember this: the minister must not be present on Thursday morning when the will is executed. Can't you make him go back to Scotland?'

'How can I manage that?'

'Insult him. Turn him out of doors.'

'Impossible.'

'If you can't manage it somehow, you may say good-bye at once to your hundred thousand pounds.'

'I'll do what I can; you may be sure of that,' said Semple sulkily.

'And there's one other thing. You remember that paper of instructions I showed you? We must get hold of that. I was forced to give it to your cousin this morning, that he might prepare the will from it. He may leave it in his desk at the office: if so, I'll get possession of it. Or he may have sent it to your uncle with the draft. Your uncle may destroy it, or he may keep it, or he may send it back to the office with the draft. In the first case it will be all right. If he sends it back to the office I shall be able to lay my hands on it. But if he lays it by, *you* must get it and bring it to me. It must not be found among his papers after his death.'

'I quite see the importance of that. What I don't see is, how I can take Dr. Mackenzie out for the evening, and yet be in my uncle's room when the post comes in, to see what he does with the paper.'

'It is a difficulty; but you must try to find a way out of it. Come now, Semple, you have plenty of brains. Is there no one in the house that will help you?'

'No one—unless—I might try it,' he added, as if speaking to himself.

'Is it of any use to try to get Alec Lindsay on our side? If he would consent simply to hold his tongue, it would be the easiest thing possible.'

Semple shook his head emphatically.

' You won't get any help *there*,' he said.

' I thought as much. Well, I shall go back to the office after dinner, and hunt about for that paper of instructions. You will be on the look-out for the evening delivery, and ascertain what your uncle does with it, if it reaches him. Keep the minister out of the way; and come to my lodgings to-morrow evening.'

' At what hour ?'

' Any hour you like. But if I am not in, wait for me, even if you should have to wait all night. I must see you to-morrow night.'

Semple promised that he would keep the appointment, and, calling a cab, went straight home. During the drive he racked his brains to discover some method of inducing Dr. Mackenzie to spend the evening elsewhere, without being able to think of any practicable plan.

Fortune, however, favoured him. In the

library he found an evening paper containing a notice of a meeting in Exeter Hall which he thought might prove an attraction to the Presbyterian minister.

'Did you see that the deputation of the American Missionary Society is to be present at the meeting in Exeter Hall?' he asked Dr. Mackenzie.

'No; when is the meeting to be?'

'To-night.'

'Are you going to be there?'

'I—I—don't know. I was thinking of it. Would you like to go?' said Semple.

'If you go, I should be happy to accompany you. I am a stranger in London, and I don't care to go out alone at night.'

This struck Semple as odd. The minister did not look like a man who would be afraid to go out alone at night. However, he saw that the only way to get Dr. Mackenzie out of the way was to accompany him to Exeter Hall; and accordingly he arranged to do so.

The fact was that Dr. Mackenzie had resolved to stay by Mr. Lindsay until the will was executed, and be ready to fortify him against the attacks which he supposed the rich man's relations would naturally make upon his resolution to enrich the Free Church at their expense. After skilful indirect questioning he had satisfied himself that neither Miss Lindsay nor Miss Mowbray knew what the old man's intentions were. There remained the two nephews. As to Alec, Mr. Lindsay himself had told his spiritual adviser that he had confided in his nephew, and had made him promise to attend personally to the preparing of the will—a proceeding which Dr. Mackenzie strongly disapproved of, though he was too prudent to say anything on the subject. He was quite convinced that anything Alec could do to prevent the bequest being made would be done.

With regard to Semple, Dr. Mackenzie was inclined to think, from the young man's

30—2

manner towards himself, that he knew of his uncle's resolution; and the minister determined to do what he could to keep Mr. Lindsay and Semple apart for the short time which had to elapse before the will could be actually signed. For this reason he thought it imprudent to absent himself for the whole evening, and allow Semple to spend as much time as he chose in his uncle's room without interruption. He had, therefore, managed to make the young man accompany him on his expedition to Exeter Hall.

But Semple had only performed half his task when he had induced Dr. Mackenzie to spend that evening where he would be beyond his uncle's reach. How was he to learn what became of the paper of instructions in Beattie's handwriting, on the possession of which his fellow-conspirator laid so much stress? This could only be done by the help of an ally; and there was only one possible ally at his command.

He waylaid Laura Mowbray as she passed

downstairs to dinner, and drew her into a little apartment that was used as a kind of housekeeper's-room.

'I want to speak to you, Laura,' he said; ' and I have only a minute to spare. Are you willing to do me a favour ?'

'That depends.'

'Don't be foolish. Say yes or no. Don't you know that our whole future hangs on what may happen during the next day or two ?'

'I suspected as much,' answered Laura quietly; '*your* future, you mean. I don't see how my future is concerned.'

'Don't you ? Are not our interests the same ?'

'Not yet.'

'But they will be. Now, I only want you to do this. To-night, most likely by the last delivery, a packet will come by post for my uncle. It will contain a letter, a bulky document, and another paper, a single sheet of foolscap folded in four. The first two I don't care a straw about; but I want to know what my uncle does with the thin paper, the sheet of foolscap. Will you manage to find out this for me?'

Laura hesitated. She had no idea of being a tool in the hands of anyone; and she was not sure that she should have allowed Semple's words as to the identity of his interests and hers to pass unchallenged. Her one desire was to discover whether Semple or (as she hoped) Alec Lindsay was to be the old man's heir. But in a moment she had decided to make herself useful, on the chance of inducing Semple to tell her something. As she wisely reflected, she could get the information which he wanted without any trouble, and either tell him what he wished to know, or hold her tongue, as circumstances might decide. She therefore whispered:

'All right. Hush; I must go now. I hear Miss Lindsay coming down.'

Miss Mowbray proved abundantly capable of executing the commission which had been intrusted to her.

She listened for the postman's ring, and, crossing the hall apparently by chance, said to the servant who had answered the door-bell:

'Is that letter for Mr. Lindsay?'

'Yes.'

'Then you may give it to me. I am going to his room now.'

On reaching the old man's bedroom, she closed the door softly behind her, and going up to him with swift, noiseless steps, she said:

'Dr. Mackenzie and James have gone out, uncle; and Miss Lindsay is asleep; so I have come to you for company. Do you mind my sitting here half an hour, while nurse goes to supper? Shall I disturb you?'

'No, child, no. I like to see you.'

'I will sit by the fire, then, and be as still as a mouse. Here is a letter that the postman has just handed in. I took it from Marks as I came upstairs.'

CHAPTER XXII.

' TWO HUNDRED THOUSAND POUNDS !'

IT was past eleven o'clock when Dr. Mackenzie and his companion returned from Exeter Hall ; and after getting a little supper in the dining-room together, they parted for the night, Semple making sure that the minister went straight to his bedroom before he retired to his own. Hardly, however, had Dr. Mackenzie been left alone, when a tap came to his door. It was the nurse in attendance on Mr. Lindsay, who had been sent to tell the minister that the sick man was anxious to see him before he went to sleep.

' I've got the draft of the will, Doctor,'

said Mr. Lindsay, as his guest entered the room. 'I thought you would maybe like to see it; and as they want it sent back to-night, I had to send for you.'

The minister professed himself to be very willing to look over the draft, and seating himself by the fire, he read it carefully through twice.

'It will be a disappointment to some of them, I'm thinking,' said the old man, as the other at last laid down the paper.

'But think of the good it will do,' rejoined the minister. 'What better use can we make of money, which is, after all, mere dross, than devote it to the cause of Christ?'

'Is the draft all right?' asked Mr. Lindsay, after a pause.

'Yes; it seems to be in accordance with your wishes.'

'Just read it over to me, before it goes,' said the old man; and the minister did so.

'Now, I must get it posted to-night,' said Mr. Lindsay, when the reading was finished.

'I'll post it myself,' said Dr. Mackenzie, promptly. 'There's a pillar-box at the corner. It won't take me a minute.'

This offer was gratefully accepted. The minister let himself quietly out of the house, leaving the street-door ajar while he went to the pillar-box, which was only a few yards off; and when he returned he went back to his own room, without making noise enough to wake anyone in the house.

It had not been without some reluctance that Laura Mowbray had consented to play the spy for James Semple. Not that she was conscious of any humiliation in the matter —she rather enjoyed the excitement of it— but she felt that in yielding to his wishes she had made the tie between them stronger than was perhaps altogether prudent. In their last interview Semple had assumed that he was her accepted lover, and she knew that he had grounds for so doing. So long ago as the summer when they had been together at Loch Long, she perceived that he, as well as

Alec Lindsay, was in love with her, although Alec's passion found vent in words while his cousin's did not. When Semple did declare himself, some time afterwards, she had given him much the same answer as she had given to Alec. But lately he had renewed his pleading, and meeting with a very weak resistance, he had assumed that he was, or very soon would be, successful. Of late, however, he had had no time for love-making.

Laura had produced in his mind exactly the impression she had intended. She did not wish to accept his offer just then, but neither did she wish to send him away. Her heart (such as it was) was with Alec; but then she could not bring herself to marry a poor man; and Alec had thrown away his chances of ingratiating himself with his uncle so persistently, that she had very little hope that he would find himself rich after his uncle's death. Semple, she felt sure, would be the heir, but she had no idea of pledging herself irrevocably till the event had declared itself.

On the morning after she had paid her visit to Mr. Lindsay's bedroom in accordance with her lover's directions, Miss Mowbray took good care to be early in the breakfast-room. She anticipated that Semple would take that opportunity of having an interview with her, and she was not disappointed.

'Well?' he said eagerly, as soon as he entered the room, without waiting to bid her good-morning, 'did my uncle get the letter last night?'

'What would you give to know?' returned the girl, with a saucy air.

A coarse expression sprang to the young man's lips, but he had sense enough to restrain it.

'Don't trifle with me,' he said.

Laura was struck by the anxious, haggard look on his face, as well as by the tone of his voice.

'Why are you so anxious about that letter?' she asked.

'Don't bother me with questions now. I'll

tell you all by-and-by, if you wish it. Did
he get the letter ?'

'Yes, I was in his room when he opened it.'

'Good.'

'And I saw him take out the two papers
you described.'

'Yes ? Do be quick; some one will be
coming down.'

'He put the large one back into the envelope, and put it under his pillow.'

'And the thin one ?'

'He put it into the little desk which stands
on the table at the foot of his bed.'

'You saw him do that ?'

'I did. He asked me to hand him the
desk; he opened it, and put the paper in.'

'Did he lock the desk afterwards ?' asked
Semple, dropping his voice.

'Yes, he did.'

There was a minute's pause.

'What did he do with the key ?' was the
next question.

'The key was on a bunch. He put it

back on the table—the little one, close to his hand.'

'I must get those keys,' said Semple.

'Not through me,' said Laura, growing pale as she spoke. 'I'll have nothing to do with taking away any papers, or burning them, or anything of that sort.'

The girl was thoroughly frightened, and Semple saw that it was necessary to reassure her.

'Don't be foolish,' he said. 'Who wants to steal anything? I want to see that paper, and I must see it.'

'Well; I can't help you.'

'Look here, Laura, you don't understand. I'm trying to counteract the schemes of that villain, Dr. Mackenzie. If I succeed, I shall have two hundred thousand pounds under my uncle's will.'

'Two hundred thousand pounds!'

'Yes; or between a hundred and fifty and two hundred thousand, at any rate. We shall be able to go to Italy: all round the world, if we like. Eight or ten thousand a year, Laura; think of that! You see it's worth taking a little trouble for. Can't you get the desk and the bunch of keys out of the room, just for five minutes?'

'Impossible,' said Laura firmly. 'I have no idea where your uncle generally keeps his keys; very likely in some drawer that is locked up. You needn't think of it.'

There was another pause.

'There is one way,' said Laura slowly.

'Yes; what way?'

'Though I can't get the keys, I might get the desk out of the room. Or you might do it yourself. You see, the desk stands on the table at the foot of the bed, out of your uncle's sight. It is not heavy, quite a small thing, and easy to move. You have only to find out when your uncle is asleep, and quietly carry the desk out of the room. The nurse would never dream of interfering with you. Of course, you would have to bring it back soon, in case your uncle should ask for it.'

'Of what use would the desk be, without the key?'

Laura smiled contemptuously, but suddenly she grew grave.

'I have said quite enough,' her face said pretty plainly.

'Could you get me the desk, or let me know when it would be safe to take it?' was Semple's next question, spoken almost in a whisper. 'Think how much may depend on it,' he added.

'Why should so much depend on it?'

'I can hardly tell you.'

'Never mind,' said Laura hastily. 'It doesn't matter to me.'

She saw it might be safer not to know too much.

'Will you do it then?'

'I won't touch the desk, if you mean that,' said Laura. 'Mr. Lindsay generally takes a nap about four in the afternoon. I could easily——'

At that moment Aunt Jean made her appearance, followed by a servant with a tray, and the conference was at an end.

In the course of the day, Semple managed to take the desk out of his uncle's room while the old man was asleep ; and he had no great difficulty in opening it by means of a pick-lock, which he had borrowed. This done, he found and burned the paper of instructions.

CHAPTER XXIII.

DAVID MACGOWAN GETS INTO TROUBLE.

THE first thing that caught Alec Lindsay's eye when he went down to the office next morning was the draft of his uncle's will. No corrections had been made in it; no suggestions had been written in the margin; and assuming that the managing clerk had looked over it on the preceding evening, he was about to send it out to the law-stationer's, when he remembered Beattie's hint that it would be more prudent to have it 'engrossed' in the office.

Taking the paper in his hand, he went into the 'outer office,' where four clerks sat whose duty it was to do the more mechanical part of the work of the conveyancing department.

'Where's Hobson?' asked Alec.

'He and Graves are out, comparing an abstract,' said one of the clerks, whose name was Hill. 'Mr. Beattie told them yesterday they were to go the first thing this morning.'

'Then you had better leave off what you are doing, Hill, and engross this will.'

'Very sorry, sir, but Mr. Beattie has given me this settlement and this mortgage to do,' pointing to the papers and parchments as he spoke; 'and he particularly told me not to leave them till I had finished them.'

MacGowan's services were available; but Alec would have preferred to entrust the draft to one of the other clerks.

'When will Hobson and Graves be back?' he asked.

'Not until late, I expect,' answered Hill; 'they have gone into the country—to St. Albans.'

It was more than probable that the two

absent clerks would contrive to make a day of it at St. Albans, so Alec turned to MacGowan and asked if he were busy.

He was not.

'I wish you would engross this, then,' said Alec, giving him the draft; 'and see you hold your tongue about it when you go outside,' he added in a lower tone.

MacGowan promised obedience with more fervour than was necessary, and Alec returned to his own room.

Left to himself, MacGowan laid the draft before him and measured its length with a practised eye. There was abundance of time for him to finish engrossing it before the luncheon-hour. He was glad of this, for it was pay-day, and he knew by experience that it was very doubtful if he would be back at his desk in the afternoon.

Every month, as pay-day came round, he made a resolution that he would dine sparely, and drink nothing but water, and return at the proper hour. But the resolution had been so constantly broken, that he had no faith in his own power to keep it, and always took care, on such occasions, to leave matters so that his absence might attract as little attention as possible. More than once he had been nearly dismissed for this very offence, but his fellow-clerks were generally good-natured enough to invent excuses for him; and once, as we have seen, Alec had stood his friend.

One o'clock struck, and the will was finished. MacGowan left his seat and went to the cashier's room to receive the money that was due to him. That official, however, had gone out, and he returned discontentedly to his place.

It happened that he and his fellow-clerk Hill were not on very good terms with each other just then, so, by way of putting off the time until the cashier's return, he took the will and the draft from which he had copied it to Alec Lindsay, and got him to go through the process of 'examining' the two documents along with him——one reading the engrossed will aloud, while the other read the draft——on the plea that Hill was too busy to do it.

As he returned to the outer office, he met the managing clerk.

'Have you engrossed a will for Mr. Lindsay this morning?' asked Mr. Beattie.

'Yes, sir; just finished it.'

'If you bring it to my room, I will examine it with you. I don't want Hill to be taken from what he is doing.'

This was an unusual kind offer for Mr. Beattie to make; but MacGowan, of course, answered:

'Mr. Lindsay has examined it with me.'

'Oh, very good,' said Beattie, as he passed out of the office.

MacGowan waited impatiently until about two o'clock, when the cashier made his appearance. By that time he was very hungry, and thirsty as well.

'I want my salary, if you please,' said he,

as soon as the cashier was seated at his desk.

'It's early in the day, MacGowan,' said the cashier. 'Better let me give you only a shilling or two now. If you take it all, the chances are you won't make your appearance again to-day, and you know what the consequence of that must be, sooner or later.'

'I'll be back at three, Mr. Carter, never fear,' said the clerk.

'You had better not take it all at present.'

'I must take it all, sooner or later,' answered MacGowan in a hard, stubborn voice; 'and little enough it is. Give it to me, Mr. Carter.'

A few minutes afterwards MacGowan was hurrying along in the direction of a large tavern near the office, where he usually dined on high days. If he had not been so intent upon getting there, he would have noticed Mr. William Beattie walking slowly along, on the other side of the street.

Beattie, who knew the clerk's habits perfectly well, was, in fact, waiting for him. As soon as MacGowan entered the tavern, Beattie, with a smile on his thin lips, returned to the office. Everything had happened exactly as he had foreseen that it would happen.

In the course of the afternoon Alec Lindsay made his appearance in the managing clerk's room, and asked him if he would attend at his uncle's on the following morning, to superintend the signing of the will.

'Indeed I can't. I have to be in the Vice-Chancellor's room by ten, and I shall probably be out all the morning. Why don't you do it yourself?'

'Because my name is mentioned in the will.'

'What does that matter? You needn't witness it. Get two of the servants to do that.'

'But I have never done anything of the kind before.'

'Why, a child might do it. Ask Mr.

Hatchett to go, if you like, but don't bother me any more, there's a good fellow. I'm terribly busy.'

Alec knew that Mr. Hatchett would never dream of attending personally at so simple a matter as the execution of a will, so he made up his mind to go himself.

About five o'clock that afternoon Mr. Beattie went into the outer office, and inquired for MacGowan. Of course he was not there—had not been seen for the last three hours. Beattie struck his fist angrily on the desk before him, and went straight to Mr. Hatchett's room.

Graves (who had just returned from St. Albans) looked at Hill and grinned.

' 'E'll 'ave it this time, to a dead certainty,' said Mr. Hill.

' Right you are, Mr. 'Ill,' said Mr. Graves.

' I'm afraid we can't afford to keep that fellow MacGowan any longer,' said Beattie to Mr. Hatchett. ' He has not been here since three o'clock—drinking, I suppose. It is the same thing every pay-day, and on other occasions too—whenever he has money, in fact.'

'Dismiss him, then, and advertise for another clerk,' said the solicitor, hardly troubling himself to look up from the paper he was reading.

'I think in that case you had better write the note, Mr. Hatchett. He will understand then that the decision is your own.'

Mr. Hatchett wrote a dozen words on a sheet of paper, and handed it to his subordinate.

'Get it copied in the letter-book, and send it to his lodgings,' he said, turning back to his work.

Mr. David MacGowan was troubled by no fears of the fate which had been prepared for him. About eight o'clock that evening he was sitting in the smoking-room of 'The Alexandra,' with a glass of punch before him, applauding, in a loud, half-tipsy tone, a song which had just been finished. Care he had cast to the winds. He was not quite drunk, though he was far from sober; and, after his besotted fashion, he was enjoying himself thoroughly. Suddenly his face grew pale, and his tongue refused to speak the words on his lips, for there, calmly surveying the company from the doorway, stood — Mr. William Beattie.

A vague sense of alarm filled MacGowan's mind; but he was too tipsy to speculate on the reason which the respectable Mr. Beattie might have for coming to such a place.

In another moment Beattie had recognised him, and walked straight up to him.

' Will you step outside for a moment, Mr. MacGowan ? I wish to speak with you,' said he.

' Better say't here, whatever it is,' answered the clerk, stringing his words together as he spoke.

' Come upstairs for a minute,' was Beattie's answer, laying his hand on the other's arm, and looking straight into his eyes.

MacGowan recognised the presence of a

stronger will; he staggered to his feet and allowed Beattie to lead him out of the room.

Hardly knowing what he was doing, the clerk followed Beattie to a private room which the latter had already engaged. On the table lay two or three sheets of foolscap, an inkstand and pens, while a decanter and some glasses stood on a small side-table.

'Sit down, MacGowan; you have been enjoying yourself, I see.'

'Just for once in a while, Mr. Beattie,' said the other, with tipsy gravity. '*Dulce est desipere—in—loco*, ye ken.'

'Exactly; and I'm sorry to interrupt you; but I want to know whether you engrossed a will this afternoon.'

'I'm sure I don't know. Dare say I did.'

'Well, it appears you have made a blunder in it. I can't stop to explain it. It wasn't your fault really; and it won't make any difference if you will just copy it over again.'

'I can't—not just now; I'll do it in the

morning ;' and Mr. MacGowan seemed on the point of dropping off to sleep.

Beattie roused him with a slap on the shoulder.

' Come, come,' he cried, ' you're not too tipsy to write——'

' Tipsy ? Who's tipsy ? I'm not tipsy,' interrupted the other.

' All right, then. Come along. See ; I've ruled a sheet of paper; and I'll read the draft for you, so that you can make no mistake.'

MacGowan suffered himself to be dragged to the table ; and, once there, his mechanical power of copying asserted itself. Steadily his pen moved over the paper, while Beattie looked over the writer's shoulder, reading every word as it was written, to make sure that no blunder was committed.

Before ten o'clock the task was ended. The document was folded, endorsed in the orthodox manner, and safely lodged in Mr. Beattie's pocket.

' You'll stand a bottle of champagne, Mr.

Beattie ?' said the clerk, throwing himself back in his chair.

'Certainly ; but I'd advise you to stick to whisky. It's the healthier of the two,' said Beattie, slipping half a sovereign into the other's hand. 'Hadn't you better go home now ?' he added, feeling pretty certain that the advice would not be acted upon.

'In a wee while, Mr. Beattie. I'll drink your very good health in the first place. I look upon that as a duty. Good-night, sir ; good-night. You're a gentleman, sir. And, look here, I'll be at old Hatchett's as usual to-morrow, and you'll say nothing about seeing me here ? It's a low place, Mr. Beattie ; I'm quite aware of that—a place I very seldom come to.'

'Certainly not. It is not my business to carry tales.'

'And, I say, how did you know I was here ?' asked MacGowan suddenly.

'Oh, I thought it likely.'

'And about that will——' began Mac-

Gowan; and he stopped, trying to recollect what the other had said about it.

'Oh, never mind; it's all right. I'm afraid I must be off now,' said Beattie.

'All right. Then, good-night, Mr. Beattie, good-night.'

And so the managing clerk made his escape, while poor MacGowan returned to the room from which he had been summoned.

CHAPTER XXIV.

THE SIGNING OF THE WILL.

'I HAVE more right to be here, sir, than a stranger.' These were the words, uttered by James Semple in a voice of suppressed indignation, which Alec Lindsay heard as he entered his uncle's bedroom next day. He had come to superintend the execution of Mr. Lindsay's will, bringing the document with him ready for signature.

The old man was sitting up in bed, a table with writing materials beside him. Near the fireplace stood Dr. Mackenzie, a look of firm resolve on his face. At the foot of the bed stood Semple, who seemed to be bitterly protesting against being excluded from the room.

'Just consider, uncle!' he continued; 'I have served you for the last ten years, and served you faithfully. What have I done, to be treated like a stranger now? Alec is to make your will; I don't complain of that. Don't think for a moment I am jealous of him. But why am I to be thrust out, while one who is no member of the family is admitted?'

The old man glanced helplessly at Dr. Mackenzie as if asking for advice. But the minister held his peace.

'I think you might let my cousin stay, uncle,' said Alec. 'It is perhaps only fair that he should know your intentions.'

'Ay; so let it be,' said Mr. Lindsay, in a feeble tone. 'The whole world will know soon enough. But don't blame me, lads, after I am gone, I did it for the best. God knows, I did it for the best.'

And Semple, having received permission to stay in the room, walked over to the window.

'We must get two witnesses,' said Alec,

drawing the will from its envelope. 'Marks and the cook will do.'

'The will had better be read first,' put in Dr. Mackenzie. 'There's no need for the servants knowing its contents.'

'True,' said Mr. Lindsay; and Alec, standing at the old man's bedside, began to read in a clear firm tone.

He had nearly finished his task, when he noticed that Semple (who was still standing by the window) was pulling down the blind.

'Don't do that, James; I have hardly light enough as it is,' said Alec.

'I thought the light was in my uncle's eyes,' answered Semple, without pulling the blind up again.

'It was very well as it was; pull up the blind,' said the old man fretfully.

Semple did as he was told, and Alec went on reading.

A moment afterwards a hansom drove up to the door, and there was a loud ring at the door-bell. James Semple slowly moved away from the window, and left the room.

'You can ring for Marks and Mrs. Jackson now, Alec,' said Mr. Lindsay.

He did so; but Marks, who answered the bell, told Alec that Mr. Beattie had called to see him on very important business.

'I wonder what it can be,' said Alec to himself. 'I will be back in a minute or two, uncle,' he said, as he laid the will which he had just read on the table by his uncle's bed, and ran downstairs.

'Lindsay,' began Mr. Beattie, as soon as Alec made his appearance, 'you saw Marchand, I think, one day about a month ago, about the Walters' case ?'

'Yes.'

'Do you remember what passed between you ?'

'Nothing very important. I told you of it at the time;' and Alec detailed the conversation which had taken place.

'Very good,' said Beattie. 'Now I want

you to make an affidavit of what passed, to be used at the motion which comes on for hearing to-day.'

'But you can't use an affidavit filed to-day.'

'We can try; and I think we shall manage it. Sit down, like a good fellow, and jot down what you remember of the conversation. I've brought draft-paper with me.'

'All right; but wait until I've seen my uncle sign his will, and then I'll go down to the Law Courts with you.'

'You needn't come just yet, for I have to get a copy made, of course. If you will only sit down and put the heads of it in writing, it won't take you ten minutes; and then, while you are getting the will signed, I will drive down to the Law Courts, and get it copied and ready for you to sign when you arrive there. The fact is,' added Beattie, 'I ought to have asked you to do this yesterday, but I was so busy with other matters that it escaped me.'

'Very well; I'll just go and tell my uncle that I am detained for a few minutes.'

' It isn't necessary,' answered Beattie with some anxiety in his tone. ' The thing would be done almost before you could get upstairs. I do wish you would do it at once ; for that motion may come on at any time after twelve, and if it is lost for want of this affidavit, it will be my fault.'

Beattie's request was not unreasonable, so, sending a message to Mr. Lindsay to explain the delay, Alec began hastily to jot down the substance of the affidavit he was about to make, while Beattie paced quietly but restlessly about the room.

As soon as Alec had joined his fellow-clerk in the library, James Semple went to the drawing-room, which at that hour of the day was always empty. On this occasion, however, Laura Mowbray was there, waiting for him.

' Now's the time, Laura,' he cried, in an excited tone, though he spoke under his breath. ' Alec is safe in the library, and the will is lying on the bed, probably ; or at any

rate it is somewhere in the bedroom. You
have only to whisper to uncle that the
solicitor's managing clerk, Mr. Beattie, wants
to look over the will to see that it is all right,
and he will let you take it at once.'

'But, James, I don't like doing it. Can't
you think of any other way of getting a
sight of it ?'

' No, I can't.'

' Why can't you go yourself, and tell my
uncle this ?'

' Of course he would suspect that I wished
to read it.'

' And is it really necessary that you should
see it ?'

' Didn't I tell you this morning, Laura,
that unless I can get a sight of it, I shall
never see a penny of that two hundred
thousand pounds ?'

' Why ?'

' Because if the will is not in my favour, I
will press my uncle to revoke it, after that
minister has gone. But unless you want to

ruin me, you will go now. Soon Alec will be back from the library, and then it will be too late.'

Still Laura was not satisfied.

'Couldn't you manage to be in the room when the will is read over to your uncle, before he signs it ?'

'No, no ; that has been done already. That is—it won't be done. Now do go, Laura, unless you mean to make us poor all our lives.'

A smile that was half-contemptuous passed over Laura Mowbray's pretty face, as she glided away from the drawing-room. She certainly did not intend to be poor all her life in the company of Mr. James Semple.

In less than a minute she had reached Mr. Lindsay's room. Dr. Mackenzie was still there, standing with his back to the room, looking out of the window. Laura glided up to the bed and spoke some words in a tone so low that the old man could not catch them. He knew, however, that the visitor downstairs

was Messrs. Hatchett's managing clerk, so
that when Laura lifted the unsigned will lying
beside him, he merely said, ' Do they want to
see it ?' at which Laura nodded, and took
it away. The minister saw that she had
come and gone, but he ascribed no importance
to what passed. He did not notice, indeed,
that the will had been removed.

Laura carried it to the drawing-room,
where Semple was impatiently waiting for
her. Almost snatching the paper from her
hand, he said in a whisper, ' Stand just outside
the door and listen, in case the library door
should open,' and took the will to one of the
windows at the farther end of the room,
to read it. Laura obeyed so far as to stand
in the doorway, from which position she
could hear anyone opening the door of the
library, on the floor below.

Semple's scrutiny of the will did not last
long. Very soon he returned to Laura, with
satisfaction in his face and bearing.

' All right,' he exclaimed. ' Now, all you

have to do is to put it back again. Here,' he
added, picking up an open newspaper which
looked as if it had been brought there on
purpose, 'slip the will under this, and lay
them both on the table. When Alec comes
back he will remember that he left the will on
the table ; he will lift the newspaper and find
it there ; and uncle will never notice, if you
attract his attention, that Alec did not bring
it back into the room himself.'

Laura admired and rather wondered at
these elaborate instructions for carrying out
what she thought was a very simple ruse.
But she had no opportunity of putting them
in practice. As she ascended the last flight
of stairs, Alec came bounding up, three steps
at a time, and overtook her as she reached
the landing.

'Why, Laura, what have you got there ?'
he asked in surprise, taking the will from her
unresisting hand.

The two stood looking at each other for a
moment, without speaking.

'What were you doing with this?' asked Alec.

Laura had made up her mind. She would not confess to Alec that she had been acting under Semple's directions. It would have been equivalent to making that definite choice between the two which she had resolved not to make until it was known what share of his uncle's property Alec was to have.

'Oh! don't tell my uncle,' she said rapidly, speaking almost in a whisper. 'I wanted to know what was in it.'

'You wanted to know whether my uncle was going to leave you anything?'

'Yes; and I pretended to him that you and the other clerk from your office wanted to see it. But I have not looked at it. I have not read a line of it! Indeed I have not!' and Laura burst into tears.

Alec did not speak. It did not seem a very serious matter, but he was pained to think that the girl he loved should have done such a thing.

'Only promise me that you won't speak of it!' she cried, with clasped hands, her eyes swimming in tears.

Alec reflected for a moment. He could not see that there was any duty cast upon him to mention Laura's indiscretion to his uncle. Even if she had peeped into the will, no harm could have been done. He gave the required promise, and turned away, going into his uncle's room, while Laura, unwilling to go downstairs and meet Semple, whom at this moment she positively hated, ran up to her own room.

'What a fool I was to listen to him!' she exclaimed aloud, when she had shut the door. 'But, after all, it doesn't very much matter,' she said to herself, a moment afterwards. 'Alec thinks it was only my own curiosity that made me meddle with the will; and *he* won't tell upon me, that's certain. I wonder whether Mr. Lindsay has left me anything! I suppose James never looked; he was only anxious to find out what he was to have for himself. And Alec never would tell me. I wonder what Alec himself will get. I shouldn't wonder if he gets as much as James. Oh! I wish he had not caught me just now!'

And, renewing her resolution to wait until the will was read before she committed herself irretrievably to either of the two young men, Laura proceeded to wash away the traces of tears from her face.

Meanwhile Beattie had left the house, and Alec had summoned Marks and Mrs. Jackson, the cook, to their master's room.

The will was duly signed and witnessed, Dr. Mackenzie looking on with a grave face; and when all the formalities had been gone through, Mr. Lindsay put the document in its envelope, sealed it carefully with his own hand, and gave it to Alec.

'Give it to Mr. Hatchett, my lad,' he said. 'He should have been here to-day himsel'—but it doesn't matter. Tell him to lock it up in his safe till—till it's wanted.

And now I think I'll try and get a little sleep, for I feel tired.'

Alec took the will to Mr. Hatchett, and saw it put away in his safe, before going down to the law courts.

As for Dr. Mackenzie, after a final interview with Mr. Lindsay he took his leave, and returned to Glasgow by the night mail.

CHAPTER XXV.

MR. WILLIAM BEATTIE ACTS LIKE A CHRISTIAN.

AFTER leaving Mr. Lindsay's house, Mr. Beattie went first of all to the Law Courts in the Strand. But he did not remain there long. He took the draft affidavit to a law stationer's, and then, leaving instructions for Alec with the junior clerk who had been waiting in the Judge's chambers, he left the case Walter *v.* Walter to take care of itself, called a hansom, and told the cabman to drive to King's Cross. Arrived there, he dismissed the cab, and plunged into a nest of squalid, airless streets, not far from the railway terminus.

After some difficulty, he found the one he was in quest of—Milton Street—and then a further search ensued for No. 76. When this, too, was found, he made some further inquiries, and, obeying the directions he obtained, made his way to the top of the house, and knocked with his umbrella at a rickety door.

A faint voice bade him enter, and there, sitting by the fireplace, was the man he sought. Mr. David MacGowan did not present an attractive appearance. Unwashed, unshaven, his shabby clothes in complete disorder, his hair undressed, his eyes blood-shot, his hand trembling, he certainly looked a miserable object. The fire, which had been lighted with damp wood under an over-burdening mass of coal-dust and cinders, was slowly going out, but MacGowan had not sufficient energy to try to make it burn. His miserable breakfast stood untasted on the table, upon which lay an open letter. When he saw who his visitor was, he did not say a word, but turned his face to the smouldering fire, and gazed at it moodily.

Beattie, without waiting for an invitation, sat down opposite him, and began to ask him where he had put certain papers which had been in his charge, and some other questions of a like nature. MacGowan sullenly answered him, without removing his eyes from the fire.

'When I looked over the letter-book this morning,' said Beattie, when these matters had been discussed, 'I was sorry to see a letter of Mr. Hatchett's telling you that you need not come back again.'

'Ay! I dare say ye ken a' aboot it,' said the other.

'If you mean that it was my doing, you are quite mistaken,' said Beattie hastily. 'Mr. Hatchett decided upon it himself; and really, you know, MacGowan, you can't be very much surprised at it.'

MacGowan gave an indifferent kind of sigh, as much as to say that it mattered little from whose hand the blow had fallen, and that he did not very much care.

'Will they give me a character?' he asked suddenly, turning his eyes for the first time on his visitor.

Beattie shook his head mournfully.

'You might write me one yoursel',' suggested the ex-clerk.

Beattie shook his head still more decidedly.

'Unless I used the firm's name, it would be of no use,' said he; 'and if I did, it might be as much as my place is worth.'

The gleam of hope died out in MacGowan's watery eyes, and he turned once more to contemplate the dying fire.

'What are you thinking of doing?' asked Beattie after a pause.

'Nothing.'

'But you must do something, or starve.'

'I don't care.'

'Oh, nonsense, man! I'll tell you what you ought to do—emigrate! In a new country, where there are fewer public-houses than there are in London, and no temptations to spend money, you might make a fresh start, and end by becoming a rich man.'

MacGowan made no answer.

'Come, now; wouldn't it be the most sensible thing to do?'

'May be; but how can I go abroad? I haven't enough to pay fare to Aberdeen, let alone America.'

'Get your friends to lend you enough to pay your passage-money, and to start with.'

MacGowan gave a scornful laugh.

'Where may they be, I wonder?' said he.

'Well, MacGowan,' said Beattie, speaking very slowly and deliberately, 'you know we Scots should help one another in a difficulty; and if I thought you would pay me back again, I wouldn't mind giving you the means of making a fresh start.'

'Would you really, man?' exclaimed MacGowan, looking up eagerly in Beattie's face.

'I would, if I thought you would really make an effort to repay me.'

'I would pay you back, as sure's death,' said MacGowan earnestly.

'I wouldn't advise any young man to go to America,' said Beattie. 'There are more men there than there is work for. Australia—Western Australia—that's the place for a young fellow of talent and energy.'

'It's a long way off,' said MacGowan doubtfully.

'Not in these days of big steamers,' said Beattie in a cheerful tone, taking a newspaper from his pocket as he spoke. 'See here, man,' he added, running his eye over the shipping advertisements, 'here's your chance: "Steam to Australia. The *Tasmania*. Third-class passage, £13. Superior accommodation." Sails to-morrow. What do you say to that?'

'It would be cheaper to go to the States,' said MacGowan, reaching out his hand for the paper.

'But you would have no chance in the

States,' answered Beattie. 'It would be throwing away money to go there.'

'I would want an outfit,' said MacGowan.

'Not very much. I'm told you can buy most things as cheaply out there as in this country. If you like to go to Western Australia, which is the country I recommend, decidedly, I'll lend you enough for the passage-money and some clothes, and twenty pounds to start with. What do you say to that?'

MacGowan was astonished.

'Man, Beattie, you're acting like a Christian,' he said solemnly, as he stretched out his hand.

Then he began to weep.

Beattie took the outstretched hand, though it was not a very clean one, and shook it.

'Look here, now,' said he, 'this is what you'll do. Make yourself as smart as you can, and meet me at the King's Cross Metropolitan Station in an hour's time. I will have half the money—twenty pounds—

ready for you then. Thirteen of that will be for your passage-money, and the rest for clothes. Go to the owners' office in Fenchurch Street, and take your ticket this afternoon. Bring it to my lodgings any time this evening, and I'll see you off to-morrow afternoon, and give you the other twenty pounds. Will that suit you ?'

'Couldn't be better, Mr. Beattie ; couldn't be better. But if the same firm should have a boat for Canada, for example——'

'I thought we had settled that,' said Beattie quietly. 'Why should I throw away my money in helping you to emigrate to a country where I feel convinced you would starve ?'

Whereupon MacGowan protested his perfect readiness to go to Australia, and Mr. Beattie departed.

Once or twice during the interview Beattie had been tempted to make distant references to what had passed at the tavern the preceding night, with a view to ascertaining how much

or how little of it MacGowan remembered.
But he wisely refrained from doing so. The
clerk seemed to have forgotten the piece of
extra work which Beattie had persuaded him
to do, or, if he remembered it, he apparently
thought it was not worth alluding to. To
refer to it now, Beattie considered, might
only have the effect of refreshing his memory,
whereas, if nothing happened to recall the
incident which had taken place when he was
half tipsy, it would probably fade altogether
from his recollection.

An hour later, MacGowan presented himself at the rendezvous at King's Cross. He
had evidently made a great effort to look
respectable; but he still had the appearance
of a man who was just recovering from a
debauch. Beattie did not detain him long.

'Here's the money,' he said, slipping a roll
of sovereigns into his hand, ' and you'll repay
me out of the first money you can con-
veniently spare.'

'I'll work my fingers to the bone; I'll

live on bread and water——' began Mac-
Gowan.

'I don't ask you to do that,' said Beattie
quietly, as a satirical smile crossed his face.
'You have plenty of time to go to Fenchurch
Street and take your ticket, before the office
closes. I will expect you at eight, at my
lodgings, to hear how you have got on.'

At a few minutes past eight MacGowan
made his appearance at Beattie's rooms. He
was sober, but to Beattie's shrewd eye it was
evident that he had been taking something
in honour of the impending change in his
fortunes. This, however, was only what
might have been expected.

'Have you got your passage-ticket?' began
Beattie, rather sharply.

'Yes, sir,' answered MacGowan, handing
over a piece of paper. 'I took it——'

'Why, how's this?' exclaimed Beattie;
'this ticket is in the name of P.
Macartney!'

'I was telling you, sir,' answered

MacGowan in an injured tone, 'that I
thought it better to take another name,
and——'

'And make a completely fresh start?
Quite right. You showed great good sense
in doing that, MacGowan. Much better to
break with the past altogether. But why on
earth did you take an Irish name, when
everybody can see you are a Scotchman?'

'It's a Scotch name, too,' answered
MacGowan, in a slightly offended tone. 'It
was my mother's name. And my grandfather
was called Peter.'

'Oh, very well; I don't suppose it very
much matters,' said Beattie, handing him
back the ticket. 'When does the steamer
sail?'

'To-morrow afternoon or evening, sir. We
are to be on board by four o'clock.'

'I'll come down and see you off. St.
Margaret's Dock, isn't it?'

'Yes, sir; but it's an awkward place to get
to, and a long way. I could call on you, Mr.

Beattie, at any place and hour you choose to appoint.'

' No, no,' said Beattie, smiling. 'I'll meet you at the ship. Will you take a glass of wine before you go ?'

'Nothing, Mr. Beattie ; nothing for me,' said MacGowan, with a deprecatory wave of the hand, turning away his head, as if to avoid the very sight of temptation. And so he took his leave.

'Arrant humbug !' exclaimed Beattie, as his visitor left the house. ' He'll go straight to a public-house. And he'll drink himself to death within a month after he lands. Perhaps it would have been better if I had given him a little money ; but sooner or later it comes all to the same thing.'

David MacGowan was waiting for his bene-factor, as the latter drove down to St. Margaret's Dock the following afternoon.

' That's the steamer, is it ?' said Beattie ; ' and a fine ship she is. I almost wish I were going to Australia too, by Jove !'

MacGowan grinned faintly, as if the treat of having Mr. Beattie as a companion were too good to hope or pray for; and Beattie plunged his hand into his pocket.

The hoarse cry of the steam fog-whistle was already sounding for the last time.

'There's the money I promised to lend you,' said Beattie. 'Count it, and see that it's all right.'

'No need to do that, sir,' murmured Mac-Gowan.

'I hope you'll make a good use of it, and —prosper, you know. Good-bye.'

MacGowan, after many expressions of gratitude, went on board, and the steamer, which was already crawling at a snail's pace past the wharf, slowly worked her way to the entrance at the further end of the dock. With the help of her tug she got quickly through the dock-gates, and Beattie stood watching her as she glided out into the river, until she was hidden in the sea-mist and the gathering darkness.

CHAPTER XXVI.

THE RICH MAN DIED, AND WAS BURIED.

On a gloomy winter morning the invisible hand was stretched forth, and James Lindsay was taken behind the veil. Then hired people came and went silently. The blinds were drawn, and the house was almost in darkness. The servants, knowing that little would be expected of them, gathered round their fire and told each other what steps they would take to gain new places. Miss Lindsay informed Mr. Hatchett of what had happened, that he might seal up the dead man's desk and the drawers of his writing-table; and Mr. Hatchett sent a trusty old clerk named Drake, who had performed that service for scores of deceased clients, to do what was necessary. After Mr. Drake's departure Miss Lindsay locked the doors of the library, and of the room where the dead man was lying, and betook herself to her own room on the third floor. Laura followed her example.

Early in the afternoon Semple, finding that existence at No. 21, Claremont Gardens was, under the circumstances, an insupportable burden, wandered off towards the City, leaving word that he would not be back to dinner.

About three in the afternoon Laura crept downstairs, and finding that the drawing-room fire was lighted, she sat down before it, and wondered for the hundredth time that day whether her guardian had left her anything in his will. She wished Semple had not gone out. She would have made him tell her. She wished Alec would come, that she might ask him—it would have been some relief, some breach in the monotony, even to see him for five minutes—but he did not come to the

house all day. As it happened, he was con-
fined to the house with influenza.

An hour passed, and Laura felt that she
could not stand it any longer. She went to
the library for a book, but the door was
locked. Then she put her hand on the bell,
meaning to send out one of the servants for a
novel; but before ringing she withdrew her
hand and went up to her own room. Very
quietly she put on her hat and boots. She
knew she was committing a breach of propriety, and that was in great part the attraction for her.

Slipping quietly, with an inward shudder,
past the chamber where death held his court,
she reached the hall, and in another minute
she was in the open air. The fog was thick,
but not too thick for her to find her way.

She knew that a few streets off there was
a station on the District Railway. There, at
least, she would find some distraction; there
would be something to look at, something to
listen to, instead of the dreadful stillness in

which she had spent the day. Wrapping her cloak around her, she hurried on, enjoying the motion and the cold air, though the fog was stifling.

When she reached the station, she went to the book-stall, and, carefully selecting two novels which promised a fair share of mental excitement and a society paper, she bought them and slipped them under her cloak. Her errand was now accomplished, but she was unwilling yet to return to that great, dismal house, so she sauntered for a few minutes up and down the platform.

The place was chilly, draughty, and almost deserted, and she was thinking of returning home, when she heard the tinkle of an electric bell and the rattle of an approaching train. She stepped back into one of the arched recesses in the wall, to wait until the crowd of passengers, who were sure to alight, had gone by.

Ten seconds more, and the deserted platform was alive with people. First came the third-

class passengers — message - boys, porters,
work-girls, stout women with babies. Then a
scattered group of business men in heavy
overcoats. And among them was James
Semple. Not caring to be seen by him,
Laura stepped back as far as she could, but
she was in no danger, as she was in the
shadow, and her veil was down.

A man whom she did not recognise joined
Semple. They seemed to have been travelling by the same train without knowing it.
The two men passed her, walking slowly on
account of the crowd, and conversing together
as they went.

'And Alec Lindsay is ill?' she heard
Semple say to his companion.

'Yes; a bad cold, he says. I hope he
won't be able to leave the house for a week,'
was the reply.

'Why?'

'Ah! you don't understand. You think
we are in sight of land. Not yet. In
fact——'

Laura could hear no more, for Semple and Beattie (who was his companion) had passed her. But her curiosity was excited. She mingled with the crowd, and managed to get a little nearer to the speaker. But Beattie had dropped his voice, and she could only catch the words—'must not be there when the will is read, on any account,' when the two men reached the door of exit, and passed beyond her hearing.

There was nothing Laura Mowbray loved so much as a secret. Here was one, she felt sure. Who was not to be present when the will was read? Alec Lindsay? They had been talking of his illness just before. Why should he not be present at the reading of the will? It could make no difference to any-one, surely, whether he was there or not. Who was this stranger who was interested in Mr. Lindsay's will?

There was no solution, however, to these questions; and Laura, after waiting a few minutes to avoid any chance of meeting

Semple in the street, made the best of her way home.

Semple, she found, had not arrived; nor did he return until late in the evening. Miss Lindsay, fortunately, was still upstairs. As the evening advanced, however, she came down, and ordered tea, in lieu of dinner, for Laura and herself. Then she went to the library and fetched two volumes of sermons, one of which she gave to Laura, while she sat down to study the other. One by one the slow hours went by, till nine o'clock struck, and then Laura went to bed, where she lay reading ' The Mystery of the Manor House,' till the cold compelled her to lay the book down.

Next day the dressmakers came with the half-finished mourning dresses, and that was a great relief ; and so the time passed until the day of the funeral.

It was a small and a melancholy company. Mr. Hatchett was there, Mr. Beattie having told him that the estate was a large one, and it would be well that he should be on the

spot. The physician was there; also Mr.
Andrew Simpson and Mr. Nicol Carnegie,
two old friends of Mr. James Lindsay's whom
he had named as his executors, and James
Semple, of course. Alec Lindsay was not
sufficiently recovered for the doctor to allow
him to attend the funeral; and his father was
deterred from making the long journey to
London by a sharp attack of rheumatism.
Dr. Mackenzie, however, had come from
Scotland, as well as a Dr. George Adamson,
who was one of the trustees for the Free
Kirk.

The clergyman at the cemetery hurried
over the last words of the prayers. Another
funeral was due in ten minutes, and the
curate was anxious to warm himself thoroughly at the fire in the clerk's office before
he began to read the service for the fourth
time that day.

Soon the dismal task was ended. James
Lindsay was laid in his native dust; and the
mourners felt relieved as they mounted the

steps of the mourning-coaches, to be driven back to the house.

When they had all taken their seats in the dining-room, which felt chilly in spite of a roaring fire, wine and cake were handed round, while Mr. Hatchett, who had brought the will in the pocket of his overcoat, made a formal search among James Lindsay's papers for another testament. He was still busy in the library when Miss Lindsay and Laura entered the dining-room.

Miss Mowbray walked slowly, with downcast eyes. She knew that her mourning dress was very becoming to her, and she secretly determined to be often in mourning, or half-mourning, at least, in the future. Dr. Mackenzie met the two ladies, and conducted Laura to a seat; while Mr. Carnegie, an old acquaintance of Miss Lindsay's, came forward and led her to a chair.

'This is a very sad event, Miss Mowbray,' said Dr. Mackenzie, seating himself.

'It is indeed,' answered the girl in a subdued tone, lifting her eyes for a moment to the minister's face.

'And it is one which may happen to any of us at any time. It is well to be prepared.'

'Oh, I am sure Mr. Lindsay was prepared to die. He was so resigned, so peaceful towards the close.'

This was said in Laura's sweetest tone, but it was not a satisfactory answer in the ears of the Scottish Doctor of Divinity.

'There is a false peace as well as a true peace, Miss Mowbray,' he said somewhat severely. 'I believe Mr. Lindsay's peace was well founded. He knew the way of salvation. But a mere general trust in the goodness of God is worthless—utterly worthless.'

This startled Laura, and, anxious to re-assure the minister, and to prevent the conversation taking a more personal turn, she said :

'I have been reading such beautiful sermons

in a book Miss Lindsay gave me. I am sure you would like them. They are by a Mr. Robertson.'

'You don't mean Robertson of Brighton?'

Laura saw that she had made a mistake.

'Ye—yes; I think so.'

'Poison! Rank poison!' cried the minister, unconsciously raising his voice. 'I cannot understand Miss Lindsay putting such a book into your hands, or into the hands of any young person. I trust you did not agree with that writer. But he is most seductive, especially for the young. Did you read many of the sermons?'

'No.' (This was true enough. Laura had read about a page and a half of one of them.) 'And I will not read any more of them, since you do not approve of them. Have you published any sermons, Dr. Mackenzie?'

'I did—some time ago.'

'I *thought* I had seen them somewhere,' said Laura, knitting her brows as if she were making a great effort of memory. ' I wish I knew where I could get a copy.'

' I will send you a volume of them, if you like,' said the minister.

' Oh, thank you *so* much !' replied Laura, with a look of gratitude.

' How we misjudge people,' said the minister to himself. ' I had thought this young lady had been of a rather frivolous disposition ;' and he helped himself to another glass of port.

As he did so, Mr. Hatchett opened the door, and proceeding to the top of the long table, amid a universal silence, took his seat.

' There seems to be no document of a testamentary character, ladies and gentlemen. among the papers of the deceased. This is a will which he executed a few weeks ago. It was drawn and engrossed at my office. With your permission I will read it to you.'

When the lawyer finished his preface, everybody assumed an attitude of polite in-difference, listening intently all the while. Laura, who had not expected to understand much of it, found that it was quite intelligible. Her own name was among those of the legatees.

' And I leave and bequeath to my ward, Laura Mowbray, the sum of two thousand pounds.'

' Well, it is always something ; with what I have I shall be independent, at any rate,' said Laura to herself.

Then came one or two other small legacies, and then the lawyer proceeded :

' And I leave and bequeath to the person who shall be the Moderator of the Free Church of Scotland at the time of my death, and to all the persons then surviving who shall have filled that office, and to every person who shall hereafter fill that office, the sum of five thousand pounds in trust——'

A hoarse, inarticulate cry had burst from Dr. Mackenzie's lips.

The lawyer stopped and looked at him.

' Read that again if you please, sir,' said the minister, in a hard, stern voice.

Mr. Hatchett eyed him for a moment before he bent again over the paper.

'And I leave and bequeath to the person who shall be the Moderator of the Free Church of Scotland at the time of my death, and to all the persons then surviving who shall have filled that office, and to every person who shall hereafter fill that office, the sum of five thousand pounds in trust for——'

'There is some mistake here,' said Dr. Mackenzie, rising and going up to the table.

The lawyer contemptuously pushed the paper under the minister's eyes and pointed silently to the words. Yes; there they were plainly—five thousand pounds. Dr. Adamson came up behind, and having with trembling fingers put his spectacles on his nose, he peered into the paper, and satisfied himself that the words were 'five thousand pounds' beyond any possibility of doubt.

Dr. Mackenzie was trembling with anxiety and passion. It was not only that an annual sum which would have doubled his income was lost to him; nor was it only the injury done to his Church that moved him; he felt that both he and the cause which he had at heart had been shamefully defrauded.

He looked at the signatures of the witnesses. They were, or appeared to be, the same as when he had seen them affixed. The date was correct. There was no appearance of erasure, no possibility that the words had been tampered with.

While the minister had been examining the will there was a deep silence. He now laid it on the table, and leaning one hand upon it, said in a grave tone :

'All I can say is that my deceased friend expressed his intention to me of leaving half a million of money to the Church of which I am a member. He consulted me on the subject. He showed me a draft of the will, in which that sum *was* so left——'

'In figures, or in words, sir ?' asked the lawyer sharply.

'I think it was both in words and in figures.

But the draft can be sent for, and it will be found to bear me out. And more than that, I heard Mr. Lindsay's nephew read the will to him before he signed it, and the sum he read was five *hundred* thousand pounds.'

'There I think you are mistaken, Dr. Mackenzie.'

It was James Semple who spoke. He had not risen. He was very pale. His left arm remained folded across his breast; with his right hand he was pulling his moustache. Laura gazed at him curiously.

'What, sir!' shouted Dr. Mackenzie.

'I only say that you are mistaken in thinking that my cousin read what you say he did. As to my uncle's intentions I know nothing.'

'Do you think, sir, that I, knowing my friend's intentions, would have heard a will contrary to those intentions read out to him before signature, without saying a word of protest, or asking any explanation?' cried the minister.

'And do you think *I* would have said nothing if such a monstrous bequest had been in the will?' retorted Semple.

'Come, come, gentlemen,' said Mr. Hatchett, who had been listening carefully to all that had passed. 'Mr. Alexander Lindsay doubtless read what was in the will; and the will is here to speak for itself. I think I had better finish reading it.'

He did so, and when he had finished, Dr. Mackenzie said excitedly :

'We do not accept that document as a true exponent of the testator's wishes. We protest—eh, Dr. Adamson?—we protest against it. We shall appeal to the law-courts.'

'Very good, gentlemen,' said Mr. Hatchett politely; 'all shall be done in a correct and orderly manner. You will select your own solicitors, whom I shall be happy to meet. Meanwhile, Mr. Carnegie, and Mr.—er— Simpson, you accept the executorship and trusteeship, as I understand?'

The two gentlemen, who knew enough of

the world to know what this meant, yielded a melancholy assent. Miss Lindsay, seeing that there was no need for her further presence, made a sign to Laura Mowbray; and the two ladies left the room together.

'And I will apply for probate, I presume, in the usual way,' remarked Mr. Hatchett, rubbing his hands gently, with much inward satisfaction.

'I have one suggestion to make, gentlemen,' he said, ' before we separate. I believe the domestics who signed the will as witnesses are in the house. It would be well to summon them now, before they have been led to suppose that anything can depend on what they may have to say, and ask them in your presence whether they can swear that these are their signatures.'

The suggestion was received with a murmur of applause, and some one rang the bell. Meantime, Dr. Mackenzie asked a question.

'If I remember aright,' he said, ' the

other legacies bequeathed in the will are of comparatively small value, perhaps not more than twenty or thirty thousand pounds in all ?'

Mr. Hatchett bowed.

' Then who takes all the money ?'

' With regard to any property not specifically mentioned,' said Mr. Hatchett, glancing once more at the document before him, ' it goes to the residuary legatees.'

' And they are ?'

' Mr. Alexander Lindsay is one of them,' said the lawyer, while a grave look came into his face.

He was stopped by the entrance of the servants, and James Semple was glad, somehow, that Mr. Hatchett did not go on to recite his name. It would have weakened the effect of his contradiction of the minister's recollection, although, of course, the whole world must soon know how the matter stood. But as the words ' Mr. Alexander Lindsay is one of them' fell from Mr.

Hatchett's lips, a certain thrill ran through the little company.

The servants declared without hesitation that the document before them was the one they had signed, that and no other ; and then everybody rose up and prepared to go.

Miss Lindsay went up to Dr. Mackenzie as he passed into the hall, with the intention of offering him hospitality, but as she was on the point of speaking to him, Semple interrupted her, affecting not to see the minister, and speaking in a loud whisper :

' My dear aunt, don't you think that after what has happened to-day Dr. Mackenzie would be more comfortable at an hotel ?'

The minister reddened and involuntarily clenched his fists.

To do James Semple justice, this piece of rudeness was not a mere wanton insult. William Beattie had carefully instructed him that Alec Lindsay and the justly infuriated minister were not to be allowed to meet ; and Semple thought it quite possible that if Dr.

Mackenzie were staying in the house he might get Alec's address from his aunt and go to him at once.

The minister, holding his chin very high in the air, sent for a cab, and drove off with his friend, Dr. Adamson, in search of an hotel. As they jolted along one subject jostled with the great question of the will in the minister's mind, sometimes altogether ousting it from his attention. Would it be fair, he was asking himself, for him to charge Dr. Adamson's expenses as well as his own to the trust, if it should turn out to be five thousand pounds only, as he might unquestionably have done if the legacy had been one of half a million? And if not, seeing that he had asked Dr. Adamson to take what was really an unnecessary journey to London, and considering that his colleague's family was twice as large as his own, would it not be incumbent upon him in equity to pay those expenses out of his, Dr. Mackenzie's, own pocket? An Englishman would probably not have raised either point in the tribunal of his conscience. Dr. Mackenzie not only raised them, but argued them, and finally decided them against himself, consoling himself as he did so with that remarkably Scotch proverb, ' It's not lost that a friend gets.'

But the sum could ill be spared; and the loss of it did not tend to diminish his resentment against those defrauders of the temple, as Dr. Mackenzie considered them, James Lindsay's nephews.

END OF VOL. II.

BILLING AND SONS, PRINTERS, GUILDFORD.